LOVE
BEYOND LIFE

Jeffrey A Brown

Meda Yin Media

Copyright © 2011 Meda Yin Media

All rights reserved.

ISBN-10: 1461135699
ISBN-13: 978-146-1135692

For Nana

Copyright © 2011 by Jeffrey A Brown and Meda Yin Media

All rights reserved.

This book, or parts thereof, may not be reproduced in any form without the written permission from the copyright holder; exceptions are made for brief excerpts used in published reviews.

Providence, RI 02903. U.S.A

ISBN 10: 1461135699
ISBN 13: 978-146-1135692

Printed in the United States of America.

This publication is designed to provide accurate and authoritative information with regard to the subject matter covered. It is sold with the understanding that the publisher is not engaged in rendering legal, accounting, or other professional advice. If legal advice or other expert assistance is required, the services of a competent professional person should be sought.
--From a *Declaration of Principles*
jointly adopted by a Committee of the American Bar Association and a Committee of Publishers and Associations

Many of the designations used by manufacturers and sellers to distinguish their product are claimed as trademarks. Where those designations appear in this book and Jeffrey A Brown was aware of a trademark claim, the designations have been printed with initial capital letters.

This book has not been endorsed, approved, licensed by, and is in no way affiliated with the Boston Celtics, Power Rangers, Nickelodeon, Kamen Rider, Seinfeld, Tom DeLonge, Blink-182, Modlife, Apple or Angels & Airwaves. The content contained herein is solely created by the author and all exact song references are cited between parentheses.

Tom DeLonge is a real person, but all other characters in this publication are entirely fictional.

This book is available at quantity discounts for bulk purchases.
For information, please email MyMedaYin@gmail.com

CONTENTS

	Acknowledgments	i
1	He Has the Power to Create Worlds	3
2	Visions Above	13
3	Exploring the Gift	21
4	Young Love	41
5	Life on Campus	57
6	Reception and Reinforcement	69
7	Moving On	79
8	Putting Fear in Place	93
9	Oem: the Man, the Myth, the Legend	103
10	The Quest Begins	111
11	Wish, Dream, Remember	137
12	The Quest Continues	147
13	Thepura, Land of the Free	161
14	The Great Moment	171
15	Perfect	189

ACKNOWLEDGMENTS

I would like to thank all the professors at UMass Dartmouth that made this a possible project for my honors thesis, namely Professor Waxler, Professor Eckert and Professor Darst. I would also like to thank my friends and family for their continued support and unconditional encouragement.

Chapter One
He Has the Power to Create Worlds

I awake this morning as I usually do, in a new reality. Yes, I am not like most people. For some reason, I have the ability to alter reality and create for myself a better, more perfect tomorrow. Why can I do this? I don't know. All I know is that the actions I make today, the thoughts I think, the relationships I form, and that which I secretly wish for, somehow creates a new reality for my dawning every time I sleep.

I dream a buffer, and awake in a new world. For this reason I sometimes skip-out on sleep. My parents think

I'm crazy, but it all evens out in my mind. I believe I am sane. Therefore, I am.

So what is the difference between yesterday and today, you ask? Well, today I am more physically attractive. My biceps are bigger, my nose shorter and eyebrows less bushy. Every night before I sleep I look into the mirror and talk to myself on how I would like my reality to be different. I sleep, and then poof~ I awake in the world of my dreams, the very world I desire. But those are just physical adjustments; typically I aim to alter the very fabric of the world in which we live.

I am popular, for a young college freshman, and I had many friends in high school. But there were only a few people I have felt comfortable to talking about my ability. And they would often ask why I don't dream up for myself a smoking hot girlfriend. I'd argue, "wouldn't that be a misuse of the gift?" Then go ahead and do it anyways, just for kicks.

But hear me out; that has only happened twice or thrice. More often than not, I respect this unusual power of mine and use it for a greater good. Just because I *can* do anything doesn't mean I *have* to. I could summon an endless supply of super sexy woman into my life, but since high school I have learned that that gets old, fast. Relationships with good looking chicks are great, but I need something deeper. When it comes to women, what I really want is an emotional, or even spiritual, connection.

Also, I believe that for every one of us there is some other person out there in the world walking a path of their own that will one day intersect with our personal journey and open up a whole new world.

What it boils down to, though, is that I prefer to use my power to better the world. Who do you think ended World War III? Ha! You don't even know about WWIII, do you? Of course you don't; you can't.

As soon as WWIII started, I created for us all a different reality in which China never invaded Tibet and the Americas never waged war on China in retaliation, even though the odds were in our favor. I'm too in love with Taoist Mysticism and Tibetan tradition to watch my home land fight with my dream land, so I created for us a reality where as far as you know, WWIII is a far distant thought.

However, I should say that all these realities are contained within the matrix. There is a matrix of infinite possibility, of all possible worlds and realities imaginable. Perhaps that is the 5th, 6th or even 7th dimension. Creativity could arguably just be a selection of a different world from another matrix, a world that is a little better as it inspires us to shift into it, making *that* our new reality. However, I personally feel that we create new matrices for ourselves. With consciousness, we create new quantum realms, resonances and realities. We are the creators of new possibility. New beliefs lead to new worlds.

Now, my creation powers aren't perfect yet. When I close my eyes a voice seldom visits me, telling me that one day I will develop my ability to maximum potential. I like to think of this voice as a guardian angel. I don't know who he is exactly, though, and maybe I will never know.

Sometimes he explains about how I can use my power for good, and the responsibility that comes with it, but he does not tell me why I was born this way. If I try to ask such questions, all he tells me is that the day I find love is the day I will have all the answers to all my questions. Hmm... interesting.

I am interested and willing to find true love, yes that is certain, but all my life I've had a greater urge... the urge to fully know myself, to become enlightened to an extent, as if to adequately prepare for a lifelong lover.

Tell me, what would better, having your best foot forward with a perfect presentation of your self, or meeting someone in your weakest state and going from there? Actually, the later option sounds more fun. Perhaps we could journey towards enlightenment together?

Deep down I believe we are all in this together. Life, personal struggles, joys, sorrows... how are we to get through it all if we do not have loved ones to help us through? And more importantly, wouldn't it be nice to have someone to share it all with? I cannot imagine abandoning this strong desire to fully share myself with someone, if that is a prerequisite to living this... Way of the enlightened one.

The idea of enlightenment tickles my fancy, but I must admit that it is not my goal in life. Ha, not even close. I just like to understand intriguing ideas fully. The more you get to know me, the more you realize my ambition to be just like any other young man's: social fun, good looking women, scholastic success, and time to play.

When I say play, I mean it. I live my life so freely that every day I feel like a five year old. No care in the world. Why? Well, why not? In America we have all we need. People, we live in the land of opportunity. How can life be so hard, so miserable, if we have the power and resources to change it? I know there are exceptional cases, but in general, people who have it all never realize it.

Perhaps I find life easy because of my power? I don't know. All I know is that as long as I have my totem in my pocket, the stars above and the tender earth beneath my feet, I can do anything, say anything, feel anything, create anything, and live the life I endeavor to live. My imagination knows no bounds.

Looking back at high school, the best part of junior year was learning of the Transcendentalists. My teacher had a golden Thoreau quote from the conclusion of Walden mounted on the wall: "If one advances confidently in the direction of his dreams, and endeavors to live the life which he has imagined, he will meet with a success unexpected in common hours."

This really rang true with me. All I do is live the life I imagine. Perhaps the reason I see this as the highlight of junior year, rather than junior prom and its post-junior-prom activities, or something similar, is because I finally felt like I was no longer alone in this world. I became aware of a movement of thinkers who, like I, transcend. By learning so much about the imagination and transcending consciousness, I found knowledge that I could finally relate to, and that made all the difference.

By contemplating Nature, the Transcendentalists began to understand the quantum energy of the universe in both scientific and spiritual ways. They *got* it. For quantum transformation, use Nature, the ultimate nurturer, the source of who we are. Use Nature to become something greater.

Some think to transcend consciousness they must pay for TM instruction. They can take that path, I'm not gonna knock it; I'm sure it is full of discoveries I shall never know. But for me, all I need is a thick English textbook, replete with the works of Emerson, Thoreau, Whitman, Hawthorne and others, a little time for contemplation and lot of time for integration. I learn through experience.

To transcend, a man need look no further than the source of his own mind, his own true nature. All we could ever need to know can be found within.

The way I see it, to arrive at a state of quantum consciousness, simply reflect upon the infinite. Quantum consciousness works by way of parallel processors acting simultaneously. Simply align your present frame of mind with your best possible future frame of mind, and you're good.

This is one of the few areas of public education I felt no urge to change. It was already perfect. I could leave it alone. Wish I could say the same for some of the other BS our people left behind for us. But I will not get into the realities we no longer live. I made a change, lol or series of changes, for the better.

And I'm not some know it all creator, either. I don't know the best decisions to make. A lot of things I do leave alone and let be, but the things that I honestly feel need to be eradicated from existence will meet that demise. I create, I alter, but I am not God. I'm just a young adult finding his Way. I simply do the Shift.

For my birthday, Auntie Patty thought it would be a great idea to give me a gift certificate to see Sally Bearse, a hypnotist who specializes in Past Life Regression and Life Between Lives therapy. Aunt Patty is one of my few family members who believes me when I try to explain my weird ability. She *gets* me. She takes the time to listen. She understands; she encourages, even.

Everyone else, other than the close friends who I confide in, think I'm tripping on hallucinogens when I try to explain my power to them. But that is just because I am the only one with memory of realities other than the present one. When I shift us into a new world, no one else knows of the past we left behind. All they know of are the limits of our new world.

I am curious to know what I will learn of this hypnotherapy session, though. What does Sally Bearse have to offer? Hope it's not a joke. This is one of those gift certificates that you set aside for a time when you'll most need it, so it looks like I won't be using it anytime soon.

Chapter Two
Visions Above

The stars have a peculiar shine tonight, as if glowing from within. I can stand out here and gaze into the heavens all night long. When others retire for the day at 10 or 11, I retreat to the celestial light show above.

Often I find myself star gazing for hours and hours, without tire. Even when the Sun again skims the meniscus of the Earth's natural horizon in the direction of rebirth, I will still be here. Impermanent, yet immortal. As stars are nothing more than condensed patterns of light, so too are humans. Out here, I feel at one.

In the stillness of the night I gain a certain clarity of consciousness. If ever you need an answer, this is the way to find it, for this was the way of the transcendentalist. He who transcends himself and his consciousness day after day, like the snake who casts off sheath after sheath, but at a much faster rate.

God, these stars are beautiful. Diamonds in the sky, lighting up the night. They remind me how everything is magic. I feel a strange affinity for stars, as if they are just as conscious as we are, as if they too are living, sentient beings. Beings with their own lives, cycles, thoughts and wishes. No star lasts forever. Like the human, like the greatest song, the star is ephemeral.

There is this one star in particular, brighter than all the others. No, it is not the north star. It is something different; it is different altogether. I know not the name but she is beautiful beyond measure. She is so white that she glows blue. When I look at her, and send her love, she shines brighter and I feel a warmth within. Why is that? How can this be? The only explanation I have is that there is a connection and transference of energy, a transference not limited by distance.

We are lucky here, being on the Earth. Why do I say that? Well, simply put, we have our own moon, an object in the sky that changes shape every night. Every time he appears he is a little different, slightly altered, and the Earth, consequently, is affected by this difference, seen in the tides, ebbs, flows, consciousness of creatures, what have you. How funny it is that the more light we have, the more awake we become?

It would get old if the moon appeared the same every night. Like the sun; the only time she really excites us is when she's eclipsed... when she finally does something other than radiate unconditionally all day. Otherwise we just get used to it, forgetting her presence as we go about our day.

I believe that we humans habitually need a break in continuity. Something to shake us up~ keep us on our toes. The moon does just that, and night time is all the better for it. From this break comes relief, and from that relief new creativity, new hope, new life.

The clearest thoughts and insights come when we gaze into the stars. I could gaze for hours and hours, letting my mind expand into an infinitude of universal consciousness, drifting away like shored-up seashells into a new wave, the ethers of some grand, ultimate reality.

But how can the stars do this? Is something magic at work here, something beyond our knowledge? Something about lights, on the backdrop of infinite, unending darkness, draws us in. Like getting a little bit closer to where we come from...

The more I'm drawn in, the more I see. Looking more intensely, I notice something new about the darkness. What once appeared as void is actually no void at all. Really, there is no darkness beyond the stars. What once was black now reveals itself to be deep purple. Purple like an eggplant, but sparkly like afternoon sand on the beach.

The deeper we go, the more we see. I love these hidden constellations, revealing themselves only when we are ready to see them. Behold, darkness is nothing but light!

Beneath these stars I just feel so connected, like there is something out there, something greater than myself. And sometimes, when I really get into it, I feel a form of love. I don't know why; I don't know how. I just feel love as my emotions travel through the sky, like rockets launching into space.

This feeling right now reminds me of the night of my first concert. It was some underground punk rock band, I think they called themselves Blink-482. Wait, no, that's not right. Oh, it was Blink-182. Yeah, that was it. It was a stellar performance beneath the stars that I will never forget.

Tom DeLonge, Mark Hoppus and Travis Barker have been rockin' it all night. The crowd is really getting into it. I, too, am feeling this. This is not just a rock show; this is *the* rock show.

We are all out here in a large open field as the echoes of kids on a roller coaster in the distance add to the excitement. There are hundreds of us, standing beneath these stars, dancing with ourselves and having a good time.

I look over to my friend, Adam, who brought me here. He's waving his hands in the air, shouting out every word to the top of his lungs. This is the most involved he's gotten all night. I bet this is his anthem. Yeah, this must be Adam's song.

The band is just a trio, but the music is full. They keep it simple: drummer, guitarist/singer and bassist/singer. Travis Barker has gnarly dreads. Mark Hoppus is wearing tube socks. Gross. Tom DeLonge jumps around as he strums his guitar every break he gets from the microphone.

As the music intensifies, as moshpit breaks out. Punkers run around, shoving and dancing, falling and picking the fallen up. One kid comes flying out of the pit. What a reckless abandon. There is violence, but it is friendly violence. I chose not to get involved though; moshing is for mutts.

Tom puts his guitar aside and dives off stage, taking a moment to crowd surf. Man overboard! He gets about twenty-five feet in, until the fans, hungry for more music, guide him back to the stage.

Tom gets back on deck, picks up his guitar and approaches the microphone. He announces that they are to play one more song. This is not what I want to hear. I'm having so much fun! Don't tell me it's over, noooooo...

But the truth is, Mark, Tom and Travis are just about done. Well, I guess this is growing up.

When the music dies, the stars still shine.

Chapter Three
Exploring the Gift

After a night of intense star-gazing and musical nostalgia, I awake to a golden sun tapping on my dorm-room window.

My arms stretch boundlessly. "Ah, college!" I think in excitement. Wednesday, September 1st, 2010. First day of school! I know it may be clique to say this, but this is the first day of the rest of my life. The choices I make now will determine the opportunities that cross my path for the next four years. For that reason, and that reason alone, I love the energy of the first day.

It's a new beginning, a clean slate, a *tabula rasa*. Today is fresh, fresh as the morning dew on a perfect summer day. Today is the micro to the macro that is my life. If I can make the best out of today, all I have do to is repeat that same action and maintain that same positive attitude every other day, for the rest of forever, and in consequence I have made the best out of life. Know what I'm sayin'?

I walk into room 111 for the first time. The first thing to hit me is the size and amount of open space. This lecture hall is giant; you can probably house 200+ students in here.

Hmm... where to sit? Who looks intelligent or interesting? Who shall I resonate with on this fine day of basic goodness? Oh, I see a spot!

I find a good seat dead center, right behind the cuties but in-front of the jokers slummin' in the back row. I seat in between a couple of nerds (I know they are nerds because of their black rimmed glasses, plaid shirts, pencils in shirt pockets and graphing calculators~ note that this isn't even a math course).

Who I resonate with is important to me. I absorb those in my environment and slowly become that which surrounds me. This is a little trick I figured out: use your environment to make you successful.

Now, this is success in terms of scholastic challenge; it is hard work that takes sincere effort. If we can meet these challenges sincerely, attacking them the way the Celtics will sweep the Knicks in the first round of the 2011 NBA finals, we better ourselves both intellectually and spiritually. Consider it a *gung-fu*, if you will.

Sometimes I cannot help but feel like everyone out there is conspiring to make me super successful. Friends, foes, all of 'em. The trick is to just stay aware for opportunities and take advantage when they present themselves. And, being as this is Morph 101, I'm sure the professor already knows this. Speaking of the professor, where is he or she? It's already five of!

Just as that thought fully passes itself across my internal awareness, like a cloud liberating sunlight, the door slowly opens. All the students, well all the *awake* ones, look to see who enters. Could this be the moment? Is this be the professor?

A tall, middle-aged man with short dark hair, clean shaven face and black rimmed glasses, similar to the nerds, walks through the doorway. My neighbors must feel at ease right now, knowing that the professor is of their kind.

The first thing I notice is that all he has brought to class is himself and a stack of papers under his arm. No briefcase, no bag, no laptop, nothing. This will be interesting.

My face turns inquisitive as I wonder what these papers are. Hmm... probably papers of the syllabus nature. Five hundred dollars says it's the syllabus!

I never miss out on a self-wager. If I actually paid myself, I'd be rich by now. I've been self-betting all my life. I basically just do this (1) to entertain myself and (2) for the thrill that comes with thinking I have won large sums of money.

He stands in the center of the room and begins to speak. I return my gaze to the professor. There's an unusual serenity about this man, as if he leads a well-balanced life style. I bet he does tai chi, meditation or something cool like that. Yeah, there's something different about this one. I sense a strong magnetism. But I like it; this bodes well for our time together this semester.

"Good morning class, I am your professor, Dr. Henry Rupert. Welcome to Morphology 101," as he walks around the room passing out papers, which I assume to be the syllabus. And I hope to be the syllabus. I got money on this! C'mon, papa needs a new pair of Macbeths!

"I assume you are all here because you have declared Quantum PsychoPhysics as a major? Wise choice, you all must be..." a student raises his hand and cuts him off.

Before Dr. Rupert can acknowledge him the student interjects, "Why is that a wise choice? I'm just in it because this school is famous for its PsychoPhysics programs and it seemed kinda interesting to me after I read these books 'Matrix Energetics' and 'The Physics of Miracles' in high school, which essentially explain how the human being and all forms of thought are 100% light on the sub-atomic..." the professor cuts him off, mirroring the student. What justice.

"Well, what are you doing in a 101 class?" He scolds compassionately. "I'm teaching a 400 level seminar right now, 'Quantum Transformation of the Bio-energetic Self' and those Richard Bartlett books happen to be part of the required reading material."

"Aw no way!" The student erupts, almost falling out of his chair as the people around him chuckle. The papers finally gets to me. It is the syllabus. I knew it, I knew it! Five hundred big ones, yes!

"Way." Reacts Dr. Rupert, calmly. "Now, stop disturbing the class. If you would rather be in that course than this introductory one, I will give you a permission number. Clearly, you have the zest of senior students at that level. I'm sure you can handle it. Meet me in my office this afternoon." The student stands up and walks out the room. That is the last I ever saw of him.

With his tone of voice, Dr. Rupert now directs his attention to the rest of the class, including the half that is still asleep at this bright time of 0800 hours. "Now, for the rest of you. This is only day one of your freshman year. It is time to learn the basics. Let me ask..." he pauses, as if cultivating an epic question. "Who here knows what it means to be a Quantum PsychoPhysicist?"

A semi-attractive girl two rows in front of me with bleach-blond hair raises a hand decored in sky blue fingernails.

"Yes, you," the professor addresses. "The Hillary Duff look-a-like." The class chuckles at his comparison, for she actually bares a striking similarity to Miss Lizzy McGuire. Yeah, she's a cutie.

A lovely, high pitched voice fills the air. "Um, actually, my name is Lauren."

"Ooooh, burn!" some of the jokers from the back remark. Dr. Rupert is unwavered.

Lauren continues, "So like, it means to understand all psychological activity... umm..." she's hurtin', "on both the physical and quantum levels, like, to the point where like..." epic fail, "one understands that all mental behavior occurs in the 4th dimension beyond space and time, and like, that thoughts reoccur in the present moment when they are like, taking us into the next morphic unit," ending her monologue with a high intonation, as if proud of that answer.

"Yeah..." Dr. Rupert encourages her. "That's part of it. Anyone else have like, something to add?"

I burst out laughing as he just mocked Lauren, possibly beyond her knowledge and comprehension. Being the only one who reacted to his joke, he immediately looks at me. Dammit. Mustering confidence, I raise my hand and prepare to wing an answer. Improv, gotta love it.

"Yes, you with the cool hair," he says, pointing at me.

Nice, he has style. And he likes my Kit Taylor cut. I take a calming inhalation through the nose and collect myself before speaking. I can use any contemplative moment I can get here. The trick to improv is centering the self before action.

I start off my answer naturally, using the question to make it sound longer and more developed. "Well," I begin, "to be a Quantum PsychoPhysicist means to have an added insight into all the processes occurring within every living thing, especially those things that involve our direct sensory experience."

"Go on," he pleads.

Time for more BS. "How we relate to phenomena and stimuli changes when we think differently of it or focus on it... our thoughts, projected auditorily, or even silently, alter matter and atomic structure... the physics of the world around us expand when we think holistically and allow our consciousness to transcend beyond normal space-time parameters which subsequently..." He interrupts me.

"Care to share with the class how consciousness transcends beyond the normal, waking-sleeping-dreaming stages that most people never surpass?"

I giggle deeply as carbon dioxide leaves my diaphragm and exits a smiling mouth. "I wish I could explain it..." I'm flattered. "I don't know, it's just... it's like... one minute you're in normal consciousness mode, minding your own business, thinking of your girlfriend or the Celtics or ninja turtles or something, then some outside force instantly reminds you of the vastness of all things, of the eternal, infinite universe within and

BOOM! Transcendence," I explain. "Catch my drift doc?" I add, hoping he understood.

"That is Doctor, not doc," he retorts, "Dr. Rupert. Henry Rupert. Please, treat me with respect as we are in a professional educational setting."

"I'm sorry, this is my first day as a college student."

"Well, I forgive you. Thanks for speaking. Hope to hear more from you throughout the semester. Judging by that answer, something tells me that you will make brilliant contributions to our field. Class, what this fine young man just did was shift gears from one matrix to another." Oh my God, he's right. I didn't even realize that with my explanation I did a little shift. "And only those of you who were awake, truly awake, came with us for the ride to the next matrix, to the next set of transcendent realities. I love this stuff!" Dr. Rupert's shift in tone to a more emotional, social state of expressing his love for transcendent matrices surprises me. I thought he was always composed, but I guess he has his moments.

A confused student raises his hand. "But, how do we transcend reality? I don't get it."

Dr. Rupert calmly explains, "By naturally living within reality we transcend its various stages. The true key to transcendence is letting the subconscious do the work as you go about your life as you most naturally feel inclined. Resonance, from the quantum perspective, is all about making the unconscious conscious. Now, any more questions?"

The room goes silent. Apparently not. I gaze down at the syllabus, or should I say, my five hundred dollar bill.

I hear a whisper in my inner ear, of a vaguely familiar voice, a voice that is not mine.

Do you believe everything happens for a reason?
The minute you close your eyes, do you see the future?
And if you could escape from your past,
Would you be ready for the next adventure?
(The Adventure / Down)

I shake it off, not knowing where it came from. I love it, though. I rip my notebook and pen out of my backpack and slap them on the desk, quickly turning to a blank page.

Fervorously I write down the message. It seems so legendary, so epic, so fitting for today's notes. The consciousness of its source is enlightened, that I know for sure. But more importantly than it being an enlightened thought, it is an inspiring thought that makes me want to take action.

But where did it come from? What was that inner whispering?

I remember seeing this on TV once, either on History or Discovery, something about ethereal beings and good aliens trying to communicate with us telepathically like this. The kicker is that they can only do this when we are of a certain state of consciousness, at a certain level of enlightenment ourselves where we are receptive to telepathic input.

But is that real? Could it be an angelic presence? And if so, why only now? Why only today do I get these auditory treats? These messages are much more direct than anything of the past.

Maybe I have shifted? Wait, now that I think of it, I have felt a little different today. Haha, well, last night before sleeping I did tell myself I wanted a legendary first day of class, a day I would never forget. And Dr. Rupert surely helped with that. But I also feel drawn to talk to Lauren, for a reason I do not yet know. And this message I just got... what next adventure?

After spending some time explaining the syllabus and his expectations for the course, Dr. Rupert dismisses the class. I pack up my things and become just another freshman walking out of the lecture hall.

Walking out of room 111, I find myself right behind Lauren. I sense an opportunity to talk to her opening. What should I say though? It has to be something good, something funny, something to help me stand out. Just as we take a few steps into the hallway, some dude in a letterman's jacket sneaks an arm around her.

"Hey Chad!" she says to him, caught off guard, as she gives herself to him fully. My chance to say something fades as they walk off together. So much for that.

I'm in the mood to experience the campus a bit. I walk out of the lecture hall building, down some stone stairs and around the corner of an unexplored building. I find a quite spot in the large amphitheatre right outside the library. The geometry of this structure is magnificent.

Ascending layers of grass and cement-stone steps, I feel like an ancient Greek coming closer and closer to Heaven. I seat myself at the apex, a man-made mound covered in grass, with a perfect view of a large open field, tree-line and clear blue sky.

Sitting here and taking it all in, I can't help but remember the first time I discovered my reality-altering gift. I was four years old and in preschool. It was around Christmas time, right after my birthday, and our class was doing a yankee swap.

Now, I did not know what a yankee swap was. All I knew was that when Mom brought me to the store I got to pick out a toy, any toy I wanted! I was so excited; I put all my thought into which toy to get. Standing there in front of the action figures, I asked myself, which one do I *really* want?

After an intense decision process, I finally settled on the Super Shredder action figure from the second Ninja Turtles movie, Secrets of the Ooze. I was so happy to have gotten this toy, so pleased with my decision. As I sat in the backseat with the Bradley's bags next to me, all I could think about was what it will be like to tear him out of the package and maneuver those plastic limbs the first second we get home.

But then something strange happened. When we got home I was not allowed to open it. This doesn't make any sense. And then it gets worse! The next day, Mom tells me to give the toy, unopened, to my teacher when I get to school.

"That's strange," I think, the next day in class. "Why is the teacher collecting everyone's toys?"

Having now collected everyone's toys in a sack, she walks around the room pulling out items and handing them to the kids, but they are all getting toys different than the ones they brought!

All I get is a lousy three-pack of 2-inch play-dough buckets :(! I went on to remember this as the most traumatic, emotionally charged day of my childhood. I was four, but it didn't matter. Something I thought was mine was taken from me; I was jipped out of something I highly anticipated.

That night I cried myself to sleep. My older brother, who slept in the bunk below me, asked what was wrong. I told him everything, from all the thought I put into selecting a toy, to looking forward to playing with it the whole ride home from Bradley's, to having to give it up at school.

He told me something I have never forgotten. "Cheer up little man. I'ma let you in on a secret. If we wish hard enough for something, really believe in ourselves, and take appropriate action, we change the way things are."

Do we really have that kind of power? Impressionable as any four year old, I took it to heart. That night, the last thing I remember thinking was, "I wish I got the Super Shredder toy I picked out instead of the play-dough. I wish, I wish with all my might. Inner dragon come take flight!"

Where I got the idea for the inner dragon I haven't a clue, but looking back, I think it rather wise for someone of my age, at the time, to think. And I take pride in that. As I've come to study Chinese culture these past few years, I've understood an Asian belief that inside us is a dragon, waiting to be unleashed.

A flock of birds pass my overhead. I pause my recollections and take pleasure in this natural commodity. They all fly in sync, as if they are all of one mind. Somehow, every fall, they always know what direction to travel. It reminds me of Sheldrake's hypothesis, that the way birds fly together along the same pathway, year after year, is evidence of morphic resonance. All their brains are tapped into the same thought and time cannot destroy it. These birds are one and they know their Way.

I begin thinking again of my childhood story, where I left off.

The surprise that awaited me the next morning shocked me with an intensity that could tear a hole through time and space. I got out of bed, crawling down the ladder of the bunk-bed, as I usually do. Stumbling around the room, still half-asleep, I tripped over something. I picked it up. It was the Super Shredder!

But how could this be?! The day before, I had received mini play-dough buckets, not the toy I really wanted. I started screaming and jumping up and down with great excitement. Agitated, my brother wakes up. "Put a sock in it butt-face, some of us are still sleeping!"

I am so happy, I don't even care. "But it's true, what you said last night, it worked!"

"Huh? What do you mean?"

I have his attention. "That if I wish hard enough, things will change!"

"What changed? I don't get it?" My brother is confused.

I try to explain it to him. "I have the Super Shredder now! I don't have play-dough! Happy happy joy joy, happy happy joy joy!"

"But you brought the Super Shredder home from school yesterday. Mom said you won it in the yankee swap, and you haven't stopped playing with it since. I remember. Yesterday you couldn't shut up about it. And you kept impersonating his voice: 'I'm gonna get you turtles, and make turtle soup! Mwahahaha' or something like that."

He didn't get it. As I grew older and periodically reflected on that moment, I came to the realization that when I change reality with wishes, only I know of the previous realities left behind. To everyone else, life goes on like nothing ever happened.

From that day forward, I knew I had an unusual power to wish things into being. I could wish so intensely that, for some strange, inexplicable reason, everything around me would change, and everyone else changed with it.

Taking back Super Shredder was small, but that day I created for myself a new reality, a new world. And it was only the beginning. Those kids who bullied me in school, wished 'em into a different district. Michael Jordan on the Celtics? Wished him onto the Bulls. Bill Clinton's second term as president? I don't think so! Wished in Ross Perro.

Originally, Jordan played for Boston. Again we had the greatest team in the league. But after a few championships, things were getting ridiculous. I didn't want to make it *too* hard for the Lakers to catch up... we need a little competition, so I had him go to the Bulls.

In hind sight, I'm glad I did this. It felt so much better to win our next championship with the big 3 era of The Truth, The Big Ticket and The 3-Point King. After a drought of failure, long awaited success seems so much sweeter. But I must say, those few years with Jordan and Bird on the same team were some epic seasons!

My idea of bringing in Ross Perro as president, though, didn't work so well. At the time I created that reality, it seemed like a great idea. Yet, the country soon fell apart. So what did I do? Well, I simply made another reality in which Bill Clinton did everything I expected of Ross Perro. Some things though, such as sexual-related scandals, are out of my control.

Chapter Four
Young Love

Morph 101 has become one of my favorite classes. Today, Dr. Rupert is lecturing on how the Internet is a perfect analogy for the way information is organized in the morphic field.

As he opened up the class, "The Internet is one of the best inventions, and analogies, because it is simply the materialistic version of the Akashic Records, which is essentially the 5th dimension of info-energy comprising the morphic field. This day in age, we have become digital beings, and the closest invention we have to the morphic field is the Internet."

Apparently the morphic field, or the Akashic Records as it was once called in ancient times, is information encoded in specific patterns of resonance. Recently, man has invented a materialistic version of the field. Just as we have always had the ability to consciously tap into the field of pure potentiality, and psychically download information, we now have a materialistic form of this with computers, Internet and smartphones. Although the technology is of lower fidelity than the real thing, it is still a step in the right direction.

Dr. Rupert also notes something very interesting about the way resonance works on the quantum level to influence our present moment: "Because of Quantum Resonance, the future trickles down into the present. By responding to our environment, we chose a given path of resonance; we chose one possible future and actualize it as we make decisions, big or small.

"The future is like a vacuum drawing in the past and present. Our experience of this vacuum is the 'Quantum Now,' the boundless field of present possibility that we are forever in resonance with," he continued. "All we are doing as humans is playing around in a virtual reality with given selections of Quantum Resonances. How one resonates over time creates the linear, space-time frame of mind, but ultimately, behind the scenes, it is all happening Now as we select what we desire to presently become."

Apparently this involves our subconscious and will even innervate our dream life. "Information magically comes to us when we need it. This is the beauty of Quantum Resonance, especially in the case of dreaming. Great discoveries emerge from our sub-conscious if we so allow them to." As Dr. Rupert puts it, future resonances manifest in the form of inspirational dreams, both while sleeping and while awake.

Morphic smartphones, subconscious discoveries and actualizations of resonance are great, but the best part about this lecture is the announcement of our semester long project:

"Let's move on to discussing the term paper. I would like each of you to come up with a topic related to

Morphology that is of some interest to you. You do not necessarily have to tie it into Quantum PsychoPhysics yet, as that is something students in my seminars are required to do, but if you do do that, it will be good practice for when you all write your thesis senior year."

Yes, I have a feeling that this paper will be fun, if not revolutionary. Intellectual enlightenment, here I come! Now, all I have to do is think of a topic.

Still sitting here in the lecture hall, I begin thinking of how much my life is changing here at school. This first week of college has been so great. I have met so many new people, enjoyed almost all of my lectures, and decided that I will stick it out here for the next four years of my life, just to see what I become.

As today is Friday, everyone is excited for the weekend. Especially all us freshmen. Now we can really know what college parties are like. "Friday, Friday, fun fun fun fun" as my roommate would habitually say.

Dr. Rupert ends the lecture and one by one the students get up to leave room 111. For some reason I can't get Lauren, the cutie who sits in front of me, out of my head. I feel as if talking to her is the only way I'll get some sort of resolution. I don't care if she has something with that football-playing Chad-dude. I know the ways of George Costanza. I know how to out-Neal Neal.

As she is leaving her seat I get the chance to strike up a conversation with her. "Are you as stoked to write this paper as I am?" Taking a risk, exposing my passion for learning and advancing my own knowledge.

She turns to me, notices that it is I who has spoken to her, and blushes. "Well I am a little nervous about it..." she confesses. "This is like, my first real college assignment..."

"True, same for me. But we have the whole semester to do it."

Her face lightens with this realization. "Oh yeah! I feel so less stressed now. I always get stuck in the present moment."

"Getting stuck in the present? Can't be a bad thing, as far as I'm concerned."

Again I've said something to make her smile. "See, no one else gets me!"

This whole time during the conversation I cannot get over how pretty she looks. Eyes, nose, face, hair~ such symmetry, such natural beauty. Yeah, Dr. Rupert was right... she is like Hillary Duff, only cuter.

She tilts her head to the door while looking into my eyes, implying that I should walk out with her. Glad I spoke up and sparked this conversation! Who knows where this will lead now.

We extend our conversation into the hallway and ultimately outside down one of the cemented stoned pathways. I should note that she was directing so much of her attention to me that she didn't even see Chad waiting for her by the door of room 111. The instant He saw me with her a pissed-off look came over his face, and he stormed off in the opposite direction of where we were going. That's one point for our team.

I love walking these stone pathways; I've done so much of it this first week. Lauren and I talk about things freshmen usually talk about: what town you're from, why you chose this school, what building you live in, etc. And it turns out, she doesn't have a thing with Chad. He's been pursuing her all week, but she doesn't know how to let him down easy. She then brings back the conversational topic that started this all: the paper Dr. Rupert announced. "So what are you gonna write your paper about?" picking my brain.

I take a second to think. Avoiding a long silence in our conversation, I decide to just talk my way into a topic. "Hmm," I begin, "well I want to talk about transcendental states of mind, like I did on the first day, but I would also really like to incorporate the basics of Morphology that we've been reading about in the texts, especially all that resonance mumbo jumbo from Sheldrake's *The Presence of the Past*."

"So are you like, skipping the quantum physics part?" She prods.

"Well if I can find a way to incorporate that I definitely will."

Lauren pauses for a second, then looks at me, puzzled. "See, what I'm confused about is how does Morphology, all that talk about morphogenetology, morphic fields and resonance, even like, relate to quantum physics? It just seems like they are two different, distant fields of thought to me..."

I love when I can get into deep conversations with women like this, when we can actually learn something together, challenge each other's knowledge, discover new things... For me, these kind of things are a must in relationships. It shows that she has a general interest in who I am and what I think about the world.

I know exactly how to answer her question, as I once had this same confusion in high school and found my way out. "Well they are distant, distinct fields of thought, quantum physics and morphology, but the relationship is actually quite simple. Think of it: if we all resonate within one given morphic unit of a reality or energy matrix at a given, fixed point in time, any present moment for that matter, say, X, we realize that we can return to this X of the X unit whenever we want.

"And when we psychologically return to it, with full awareness, no matter where or when, it is just the same as we left it. You pick right up where you left off. Like those things you said the first day about the 4th dimension. When we return to X it is exactly the same as when we left it. Both times have the same energetic quality even though linearly they are two different, unique times in history. And why is that? Because the morphic field exists beyond space and time, even though it permeates basic, linear progression."

"Ooohh," she instantly sounds, as if starting to grasp this concept. "So you're saying that like, the morphic resonance of X is always the same, no matter what time or time again we return to it because it is of that unique energetic frequency and vibration, quantumly speaking? Like both experiences of X are actually the same moment?"

"Precisely!" I incite. "Because it is X of the X unit resonating at its unique X frequency at two distinct times from the linear perspective but the same time from the quantum perspective, because at the quantum level there is no difference between one moment of time and the next."

She looks at me, smiling. But there is an unusual twinkle in her eye, as if she had an ulterior romantic motive behind her question. Only now do I realize this. Cunning girls... get me every time.

My mind wanders back to thinking of the assignment. I then explode without restraint. "Ah! You just gave me a great idea for my paper! I shall call it: Quantum Resonance and Morphology. whad'oo'ya think?"

"It's good," she pauses. "But..."

"But what? That's gold Lauren, gold!" I say, too confident for my own good.

"But it sounds like, too generic to me, that's all. Anyone could write that paper. Do something outside the box, I know you are like, naturally an outside the box kinda thinker," as she looks at me with a wink. Another flirtation; I like where this is going.

"Hmm... alright." I take a moment to compose my thoughts and settle down from the recent explosive outburst. I also need to synthesize exactly what's going down here. Does she feel for me the way I do for her? The excitement of young love? The opening of new possibility? Man, that would be sweet.

I think of a quote a friend once posted on facebook: *Each friend represents a world in us, a world possibly not born until they arrive, and it is only by this meeting that a new world is born.* That's exactly what's happening between Lauren and I right now. This is the birth of a new world.

Heeding her advice, coming back to the moment, I respond, "Yeah, I gotta incorporate transcendentalism somehow."

"Hey! how about: Quantum Resonance and The Morphology of Transcendent Thought?" She asks, bouncing an idea off me.

"I love it!" I shout instinctively, losing my cool, exploding again, as I then feel embarrassed for showing too much enthusiasm in front her. I flush.

Luckily, she is not pushed away by this. She just responds warmly and excitedly, making it all a good thing, dissolving my discomfort. "Really? Is it the title you've been looking for?" Confident in her creativity.

"Yes," I nod most assuredly. "Yes it is. Wow. Sounds so nice, so descriptive, and it just rolls off the tip of the tongue." I wavingly roll my hand into the air as if outlining the arc of a small rainbow, "Quantum Resonance and the Morphology of Transcendental Thought." My hand falls as I look back into her eyes. "I am so happy I could kiss you right now," taking another bold step forward.

She stops walking and looks me square in the eye. "I dare you! You won't do it..." egging me on with her left eye slightly winking and the corner of her lip smirking.

And with that, I turn to face her. I lean in 10% and she leans in 90. I gently close my eyes as our lips press and mold the way the peanut-butter-covered slice of bread meets the jelly-covered slice. A lovely meeting, a fantastic match.

One second. two seconds. three seconds. and our lips are still touching. I feel as though my heart is melting.

Touched by waves of a former reality, I become shy and puzzled. I think, "What am I doing? We aren't even going out but here I am at the beginning of a passionate kiss. Dare I continue?" and with a nervous quiver, that she likely felt, I open my eyes and back away. I see her eyes still closed as she displays a general face of girly satisfaction.

Apprehensive, I speak up, "Sorry, I didn't think you were serious with that dare..." as she opens her eyes with an expression of "why did you stop, jerk?"

"It's okay," she reconciles. "I got to get going to the yoga club meeting anyways, but this was fun!" She turns away and walks off. "See you in class Monday!"

We part, and as I walk away I notice a super hott redhead chick watching me from a distance. I wonder how long she has been there watching me? Watching us? Part of me feels violated, while another part feels flattered. Well, PDA. You have to expect these kind of things.

I walk home, to my dorm-room, taking a short cut down a beautiful dirt path through the trees. God, I love the woodland areas on this campus. It's like a forest but the trees are so perfectly spaced that each limb can grow to its fullest potential. I think I remember reading about this in *The Celestine Prophecy*. Instead of walking on leaves, I am walking on grass. Best of both natural worlds, as far as I'm concerned.

As I walk I recollect everything that just went down, from the thrilling lecture in Morph class to me finally breaking the ice and talking to Lauren, the great conversation we had, to my actual romantic kiss with her, and her actual wanting of more. I'm a stud, I know, I know.

And then, of course, that redhead chick watching from a distance. What does this all mean? So many women, so little time... Haha, just kidding. I never get involved with more than one woman at one time; that's just not right.

They say don't put all your eggs in one basket, but I do the opposite. If I have a chance for something, no matter what it is, I focus all of my energy on it. If it doesn't work, then I move on to the next best option. So in this case, Lauren is the only one getting my flirt energy, and if things between her and I don't work out, I just pull a Jay-Z and go on to the next one.

I don't not take advantage of unique opportunities, usually, such as kissing Lauren. I mean, come on, I've had a crush on her since the first day of school when she opened her mouth in Dr. Rupert's class. Wednesday, Thursday, today... That's a whole two and a half days! The momentum was building like water receding back into the ocean before a good wave.

But still, no matter how close I come to Lauren, I imagine that I will still feel a weird void inside. I don't know why, and I don't know where it comes from. It feels like a longing, a yearning, and my whole life nothing has ever satisfied it.

What is this void? What do I do? Would it be better to fill it or let it be? Oh well, I'll just listen to the music in my head as I keep on walking back to my room. God, I wish I had an iPod.

I open the door to my building and walk up the stairs. Ascending, I naturally contemplate. I think again about the title. "Quantum Resonance and the Morphology of Transcendental Thought."

It's a great title, but now that I think about it, thought isn't what resonance is about. Resonance leads to thought, and from resonance thought is born. No, no, no. Lauren had it all wrong actually, the more I think of it. Resonance is about experience, for it is the essence of life in motion~ quantum resonance, on the level of human consciousness, is the universe experiencing itself.

Just as I approach to door to my room it hits me. I know my title. "Quantum Resonance and the

Morphology of Transcendental Experience." Yeah, *that's* it. *That's* the one. Got it! Now, time to eat a pistachio muffin and bathe in the contentment that is my life.

Chapter Five
Life On Campus

That first Friday night, my roommate and I decided to go to our first college party. It was going fine, and we were both having a good time, experiencing something new, but I could not help but notice how drab the energy in the room was. Must of been all the downward vibes emitted from the alcohol, drunk kids and general lack of mindfulness. I would consider this a rather unhealthy resonance, although it is also entertaining.

Having now been at this party for a few hours, I contemplate leaving to go outside and gaze up at the stars.

Parties of this nature get old quick for me. Like I said, I need depth in my life.

Suddenly the energy elevates. Something is now different; something is new about the overall feel of this room. The resonance has shifted. I don't know what happened exactly, but I sense a change.

I look to the door as it closes. A couple of cute girls had walked in, one of them strikingly gorgeous. I turn to my roommate, who is chugging down his fifth Miller Lite and dancing freely. I tell him I will be right back.

I make my way closer to the girls. I feel an attraction so I wish to explore it further. By exploration I don't mean flirtation; all my eggs are in the Lauren basket right now. But what I do mean is going up to the pretty one and talking casually, like friends, because sometimes we will feel this kind of attraction to people when there is something we should talk about. The Flow has this way of bringing people together.

A strange feeling of synchronicity arises as I physically feel an energetic acceleration between my third and fourth chakra. This is the beginning of another new world.

Sneak attack! I approach from behind and tap her on the shoulder. She turns, and I notice it to be the red head chick from earlier.

She looks at me, wondering why I snuck up on her, and just stares, waiting for me to say something. Just now I realize I approached a girl without priorly figuring out what I would say to her. Usually I think before I act, you know, plan *then* execute, but here in college I'm starting to learn that thought and action become a seamless activity, if done from the right frame of mind.

Adhering to the "first thought, best thought" principle, I go with the first thing that comes to mind. "Hey, this may sound random, but I think you have a beautiful presence. When you walked into this room everything shifted, and not everyone can do that. You have a strong magnetism about you. Just wanted to let you know."

"Umm... thanks," she responds as if put in an awkward situation. "Where's your girlfriend?"

"What? Oh, you must mean Lauren. She's not my girlfriend, but hopefully soon she will be," I smile. "Right now she's just a girl I've kinda had a crush on and... kissed, which I *know* you saw."

Busted. "Yeah," she admits, "I saw the whole thing. Felt like I was on the set of a Lifetime movie or something. I remember what your auras looked like together... sparks were flying all over the place! You two were really going at it. I could tell that there's a lot of chemistry and passion between you two."

"For girls like her, of that beauty, it's hard to pass up opportunities to go deeper, ya know?"

She cheers, "Haha okay playa, I feel you. I'm Alexandra," as she issues a right hand for shaking, "but my friends call me Ally. Can't really chat now but there's something we need to talk about at some point."

This is a little random, but I consent. "Okay," I say as I reach down to take my cell out of my cell phone pocket.

I look down to open up my phone, preparing to add in a new number. "What's your numb..." I say as I look up to her, only to realize she has vanished. WTF?! Where did she go?

Ally now gone, I leave the party and go out to look at the stars. It is funny to think that this here light-show is only visible when the sun, the great morning star of our solar system, retires for the day.

What would it be like if the sun were not as bright, as to leave a deep, pale blue or pinkish-purplish backdrop behind stars during the day? Would we get sick of seeing stars or would the change in background color make them more appealing, enticing, attractive?

It is all so distant, yet all so near. Where are these lights? Are they out there, or really in here, inside, within the animative force that is the human soul?

The eye perceives light and recognizes in the occipital lobe via the optic nerve where it is then cognized as light, contrasted from darkness. Yet, how else could I come to know something outside myself if it wasn't already within? When the stars through down their spears, are we the water'd heaven, the tears?

I come to the conclusion that everything experienced outside of ourselves is nothing more than a reconnection to something within. We are the distant, but also the near. All that we think to be out there is just a projection of what is in here. Well, most things. I don't know, what am I thinking? It's late. My mind in on a tangent. Nothing really makes sense.

The weeks of my first semester pass at a quickening pace. One week of lectures, one weekend of partying. Another week of lectures, another weekend of partying. One week of lectures, an in-depth conversation with Lauren, a romantic evening at the beach as the sun sets, one more weekend of Friday fun fun fun fun.

Oh, I forgot to mention. The following Monday after the first week, during Morph 101, I wrote on a piece of paper:

Dear Lauren,

You are super cute, and I've had a crush on you since the first day of the semester. Will you go out with me?

( ) yes

( ) no

( ) maybe

check all that apply.

I folded it up the way we did when passing notes to each other in elementary school and threw it in her direction. Just as I had planned, it landed right on her notebook. She looks it at, slightly startled by this air mail, then looks around to see me smiling at her. She smiles. She knows the source.

Ever since that day, we have been an item. Having a girlfriend in college is so much different than having a girlfriend in high school. No great distance across town between you, no major commitments of things to do after class, and no curfews. I could really get used to this.

Tonight there is a special event happening on campus. This guy, who goes by the name Mr. Manifest, is giving a talk in the auditorium about how we can attract new possibilities into our life, become super successful, get anything we want, yada yada yada.

Lauren and I went to the talk and it was very interesting, though I doubt he was born with the last name Manifest. But if he was, I would definitely say he has found his calling. With a name like that, you must end up where he is, doing what he does.

Lauren really liked the talk too, although I think some of it went over her head. But that is okay; that is the nature of such events. Everyone goes to a same event and everyone leaves with a different interpretation and unique impression on what happened. Kind of like religion: everyone is in the presence of God, yet everyone has their own way of experiencing it, explaining it and believing in the reinforcement. A Muslim, Christian or Hindu cannot tell me I don't know who or what God is if my interpretation is different than theirs, because simply put, I am here. I was there!

After the talk, I walk Lauren to her room and then go to mine. Conveniently, we live in the same building: Waterchestnut Hall. As I enter my room, I notice that for the first time this semester, my roommate is not in here playing one of his computer games.

This lack of explosive, army raiding background sounds gives my mind the perfect opportunity to collect itself and reflect on the talk we were just at. His words echo in my mind,

...The original pre-form of everything is vibration. Those pre-forms that vibrate loudly enough materialize, like survival of the strongest. This is the way of universal manifestation, this is the way things come to be...

...The things we attract into our life are a result of our own magnetism. To attract different things, change the way you think and what you focus on...

...Intention is energy and love, too, is an energy. With different people we experience different fusions of energy, and consequently different flavors of love...

...Intent is the engine behind conscious expression and quantum creation. When we intend and work for a certain reality to come into being, the universe responds with a given result...

...Where does sincere work get you? It takes you to your next-best future, to a more lighter, unfolded present...

...Potential is the force driving the vacuum as we project our intentions in the field beyond space-time parameters...

...If you believe it, it is so...

...Love is the only thing that sustains manifestation. It is the glue, if not the fabric, of our universe and man instinctively lives according to these laws of love. Action and love are interconnected; desire drives action and good deeds often result in the human emotional experience of true, pure love...

Some things Mr. Manifest said I agree with, but other things I do not. Yes, science has validated that everything is a vibration. But how can psychologically adjusting one's magnetism change one's circumstance? Think of the helpless people in this world, like an infant who cannot escape it's abusive parents... what could it possibly do to change that circumstance?

I only know the world through experience. The idea of love, though, makes sense; I can draw on personal experiences for that. Love has a way of making things happen.

All that in mind, I wanna test out these concepts and see if I really can manifest things.

Sitting at my desk, I question myself. What would I really like to have in my life right now? I'm gonna go for something easy, something that won't require much work. I am really inspired by the people who can just think of things and have those things appear in their life the next day, but I will take baby steps.

Like he said, all I have to do is believe it, and it will be so. But judging by his closing statement, and how he brought it all back to love, I must expect new things to come into my life while operating at a vibration of love.

I take one of my 3x3 yellow post-it notes and with my red calligraphy Sharpie write,

Dear Universe,

Thanks for the new iPod, preloaded with awesome music. It means so much to me, it has really changed my life. Much appreciated!

I don't know where to put this, so I just stick it on my forehead. Having this message so close to my third eye and frontal lobe can't hurt, can it? In a room still peaceful, I sprawl out on my bed and fall right asleep.

Chapter Six
Reception and Reinforcement

The next day passes just like any other. Wake-up, breakfast, episode of *Kamen Rider*, shower and class. What is *Kamen Rider*, you ask? Good question. Allow me to explain.

Last year, while flipping through the channels, I stumbled upon a Disney rendition of *Power Rangers*: *Power Rangers RPM*. Apparently Disney had bought the franchise in 2001 and Power Rangers has been running continuously, with new seasons, since the early 90s.

Excited to be reunited with a childhood love, I watched with anticipation. It's morphin' time!

But no. Not even close. If this is not an epic fail, I don't know what is. This *RPM* in no way compares to the Fox-aired Saban classics of *Mighty Morphin*, *Zeo* and *Turbo*- the seasons of my generation. As you might expect, I turned off the television and began forging my own ideas for what a Super Sentai series should *really* be like.

It took a few days, but finally it hit me. What if we lived in a reality where there was another breed of teen-transforming superheroes, one's who fought with passion, purpose, and individual motives? Thus began the *Kamen Rider* legacy.

I sketched out an elaborate dynasty, with an original Masked Rider hitting the public decades before *Power Rangers* were even conceived. Ten generations of riders later, in 2002, *Kamen Rider Ryuki* airs in Japan. Rather than predictably fighting giant monsters as a team every episode, these 13 riders of *Ryuki* battle one another, each with personal reasons for wanting to win a Rider War. *This* is drama; *this* is what Super Sentai should be about.

Love Beyond Life

The firm foundation of this Japanese hit made possible an American adaptation of *Ryuki: Kamen Rider Dragon Knight*. Every rider has a unique back story that develops throughout a season of carefully designed plot-twists, alliances and unexpected surprises. *Dragon Knight* has a depth that is to forever be unmatched by any kid show.

No generation of *Power Rangers* can compare to this one generation of *Kamen Rider*. This took much prep-work, but I conceived for us a reality where we can finally enjoy quality Super Sentai productions, the way adults never get sick of their prime-time programs.

But, I didn't want to completely destroy the *Power Rangers* franchise. I don't blame the writers; I blame the network. Disappointed with how Disney handled *Power Rangers*, I had Saban buy back his claim-to-fame and take it to Disney's dreaded dark horse, Nickelodeon. I await their *Power Rangers Samurai*, that is to air this February, but I know it has nothing on my *Dragon Knight*.

After class, I run upstairs to the computer lab. For some reason I feel urged to check my university email. It is probably nothing, but I am not one to brush aside intuitive inklings.

I enter the lab. It is full of people; every computer station is occupied. "Great," I think. "Now I have to wait. And I don't even really know what I'm doing here." There are four or five people waiting in-front of me, and no one in the lab seems to be leaving.

A few minutes pass and I am now at the front of the line. In the distance I see a monitor return to the blank blue desktop wallpaper. Finally, an opening. He walks away as I walk towards it swiftly. As preferred, it is one of the four computers that is in front of the large window. You know me, I always have to have a window of opportunity. Sitting at a desk without a window is like being in a room without books. It's ridiculous.

I sit down, fire up Firefox and log in. No emails. Nothing. Hmm... guess my intuition was wrong. Oh well. But now that I am here, maybe there is something else I need to be here for? Maybe that was just a stepping stone, bringing me here to do something more important.

Love Beyond Life

Desperate for ideas, I steal a glance at the computer screen to my right. Another student wasting their life away on facebook. Really? They have nothing better to do in the lab than update their status and creep on friends that they have never actually met? Look around Mr. Considerate; this is a full lab. Some people waiting in line for a computer don't have a computer at home. Well, early bird catches the worm.

I look at the screen to my left. She is modlife-ing. Now *that's* a girl who knows how to social network. Modlife.com is the future of social networking. Five years from now, modlife will be the new facebook and facebook will be the new myspace. Once it becomes a tad more user-friendly, it will have facebook beat. Modlife is designed to connect people in ways that facebook programmers could never imagine.

I consider striking up a conversation with this girl to my left, and telling her my usersite so we can become modfriends, but I decide against it. I'm just gonna go back to doing what I came here to do.

With wishful thinking I check my email once more. To my surprise, I now have an email from campus services. Apparently, a package has come for me. Is this what brought me here? I am excited, but also suspicious. I am not expecting anything? I have no orders on the way, and no family has warned me of care-packages.

I log out, leave the lab and take a left down the hallway. As I turn to walk down the open stairwell on the right, a flyer catches my attention from the corner of my eye. I pivot my head for a full view.

It is a poster for a "2012 preparation group." As it reads in bold text, "**The apocalypse is coming! Learn how to prepare yourselves and your loved ones! For a $200 deposit you can reserve a space in the fall-out shelter below our university, ACT NOW!**"

What a gimmick! 2012? Apocalypse? Bring it on.

I return to my room with this new mystery package. I am really curious about what is in it, and eager to find out, but just in case it is a bomb or anthrax or something, I ask my roommate to open it for me. At first he refuses, but I tell him that I think there are homemade cookies inside, and that he can have first dibs. He complies.

He opens the package. "Hey... there are no cookies in here!" Hands rummaging through the contents. "It's just some old, beat-up silver iPod classic with a note inside. I want my cookies, goddammit!"

My jaw drops. I forgot all about the post-it I stuck on my head last night. I went the entire day thinking about *Kamen Rider* and going to class that I remembered nothing about the intention I had set.

I read the note inside.

Dear shifter,

By the time you get this message I will already be long gone. I plan to embark on a deep space mission in 2006. However, I have loaded this iPod with life-altering music, the debut album by my new band, Angels & Airwaves. Yes, you will also find all your favorite Blink-182 and Box Car Racer classics on here. But what's most important is that you listen to We Don't Need To Whisper. *Because we don't.*

I told my wife that if I do not return to Earth by the Fall of 2010 that she should send this to you. I gave her your name so that she could use facebook to look up your current address and location information when the time was right to ship this off to you. Isn't the Internet a great resource?

I hope this is not too forward of me. Trust me, you will need this. Music bridges the gap between parallel universes. Music has the power to move the energy, a power unlike any other force I know. Sound is consciousness. Listen for the messages. It will change not only your life, but everyone else's. This may sound strange now, but in time you will understand.

Sincerely,
Thomas DeLonge

P.S. This is a magic iPod. And it is the only one out there. So take good care of it.

Tom DeLonge, you mean the dude from Blink-182? He has a serious side? Deep space... what? Don't send till the Fall of 2010... excuse me? I have much more questions now than I do answers.

But, Impressed by my ability to bring things into my life, I grasp the iPod, run my fingers along the scratches and dents, a sign that it has experienced the world, and place it on my desk next to the post-it.

I pick up the post-it and examine it closely. There is now a green check mark on it, a check mark that had not been there before. I didn't write it. I don't even have a green marker. I wrote that request on it with a red marker last night, but that was all. How? Who? When? Why?

Chapter Seven
Moving On

My whole first semester passed without once running into Ally again. We never got a chance to talk about what we were destined to talk about. But hey, this is only the end of my first semester; I'll be around for a while.

Finals week is a lot of fun though, because aside from having to take an hour long exam every now and then, Lauren and I are practically inseparable. Over the past few months we have really grown on each other. Things just get better and better.

All morning I've been working hard on my Morph 101 paper as Lauren lays in the bed next to my desk, sleeping like a baby. "Quantum Resonance and the Morphology of Transcendental Experience" is now complete. Eager for an audience, I wake up Lauren so I can read her my conclusion. She perks up and sits cross-legged on the bed, giving me her full attention.

We make eye contact before I begin. Fresh. Clear. Awake. Looking back at my laptop screen, I clear my throat.

In conclusion, transcendental experience is just that: the experience of life in the form of infinitely multiple dimensions right here on Earth as humanly as possible. Experience is living resonance. Resonance is consciousness and it operates solely on the quantum layer of reality. Therefore, transcendental experience is nothing more than living one's highest resonance.

Quantum Resonance is the synthesis of quantum physics and morphology. Through the field we remind ourselves of our true journey and through right action we re-awaken our highest possible resonance. Because energy is neither created or destroyed,

Quantum Resonance is accessible and selectable at any moment. Choose your destiny. With Quantum Resonance, create yourself.

The different places we go to, have ever been, and currently reside, are all stored within a person private morphic field, which in we resonate our soul's purpose brightly now and forever. This is the carving of destiny at its finest.

Where we live shapes our identity. Our environment chizels away at us, but our actions widle and fine-tune who we really are. Our soul's purpose lives out itself no matter what we do, regardless, because we naturally are who we have always been and forever will be. Our environment, plus our attitude to ourselves and the world outside us, perpetually re-aligns our Quantum Resonance to the life we are destined to live, and nothing short of a miracle can ever change that.

She listens for the silence to augment, awaiting confirmation that it's over. I shift my gaze away from my laptop screen to her beautiful face. I love the way it looks in the morning, bright blue eyes, so fresh, and long blond hair all frazzled.

Bubbling over in happiness, she claps ecstatically, clearly proud of my accomplishment. "I love it!"

This is another thing I like about her: when I share accomplishments and creations with her she feels my excitement. Because of her, what I have to offer to the world becomes more valuable.

The rest of our day together was great, as she, too, shared with me the conclusion of her paper before we walked up to Dr. Rupert's office to turn in our work.

Walking up the stairs to the red carpeted topfloor, in a building that otherwise has stone floor barren of carpet, I become aware of a different level of energy. This red carpet is symbolic, like anyone with an office here has reached the highest level of thought attainable. We find our way to his office. The door is open, as usual.

As we approach the door, papers in hand, he looks up from a book and greets us with a smile.

"Professor, we have the stuff," I kid.

"Oh, great," he plays along. "I was running low on... stuff... Usually I have a guy I go to, but it's better when the stuff comes to you."

Lauren and I hand him our papers. He looks at both of titles, then puts Lauren's paper on the center of his clean slate desktop first and mine on top of hers. "Saving the best for last," he discloses.

"Yeah," I admit. "I read her paper, it is ten times better than mine... not gonna lie. But I gave my paper a sincere effort and wrote from the heart."

"As expected," he responds, seriously. "In whatever you do, or wherever you are, always remember: sustain the best resonance, in any way possible and by any means necessary."

We begin to walk out of his office, heeding the advice.

"One more thing..." Dr. Rupert calls our attention. "Beware the romantic resonance. Once you love, you can never go back. The opening of one's heart is irreversible."

"Thanks," I say after a moment of contemplation. We walk off into the hallway.

Lauren doesn't seem to understand, but I think I have an idea of what he is saying. When you start to love someone you make yourself vulnerable to the entire world. But, if you resist opening yourself up to someone, you will never experience all of the beauty that the world has to offer.

Relationships on campus are interesting things. During the semester you become so accustomed to always being available and spending time with each other, then when the semester ends, you go home your way and they go theirs.

But Lauren and I kept up good communication throughout our first winter break, despite the great distance between us. Cell phones and the Internet make this easy to do. Our love for each other stayed alive; we adapted to the circumstances and made it work.

After a good long month of missing her, and that pretty face of hers, it is finally time to return to school for the Spring 2011 semester. Another new beginning, how exciting! Also, a few more weeks till the premiere *Power Rangers Samurai*. Nick, let's see what you've got!

The first day back everyone is so busy with moving back in and getting ready for class the next day that Lauren and I never got to meet up. That is understandable; we both have our separate lives.

I've always thought that one of the most important things in a relationship is finding that balance between the lives two people live separately and the life they live together.

However, the first couple of days of the semester go by, and still Lauren and I have not seen each other. I tried calling her a few times and never get through. But that's okay; she is probably just busy.

Then, on that Wednesday in the middle of the afternoon I get a text from her. I am excited now; maybe we'll hang out later. I open the message:

I'm sorry, but we can't see each other anymore. I don't think you've been open enough with me; I feel like there's something deep down inside ur like, always holding back, hiding. And I like someone else. Ur a great guy... I feel terrible... but like, it's over. No hard feelings?

Well that was unexpected. Text message break-up? What is this, Elementary school? After all we've had, and how close we came last semester, I really thought she would of at least had enough respect for our relationship to say something like that to my face.

I take a minute to think this through. Knowing this is out of my control, I welcome the end. I text back:

If you wanna try to talk this out, I'm willing to do that. But if you don't want to try, okay then, that's fine. I did all I could. Have a nice life.

One thing beautiful about the universe is balance. When one door closes another opens. When one person walks out of your life another walks into it. In one of my classes, I became close friends with a KaiZen Psych major, Jon Stevenson.

Jon and I are in "The Psychology of Buddhist Practice" together. The course is essentially about integrating Buddhist practices and Zen ways of living into daily activity while learning to expand consciousness. The overall premise is that a beginner's mind is a healthy mind, that life should be treated like a practice, with mindfulness in all doings, if we are to transform ourselves psychologically.

For the first few weeks, Jon and I never spoke to each other. He was just another student in the class to me, another face in the crowd. But one day, as I was walking around campus, working on my assigned "conscious walking," we crossed paths and he sparked up a conversation.

"Hey, you're the kid from Buddhist Practice."

"Yeah, that's right," I confirm, slightly recognizing him. "What's your name again?"

"I'm Jon, Jon Stevenson. Just out here getting some air."

I await for him to say more.

"So, practice any 'conscious walking' lately?" He says, cracking a joke and rooting the conversation in common ground.

"In every step," I come back confidently. He displays a general face of disbelief.

Time to change the subject. "So tell me, Jon, what is your major?"

"I'm a KaiZen Psych major," he responds, proud of his path. "What are you?"

"Wait," hold the phone. "KaiZen Psych, that sounds so cool! What is it about?"

"Well," Jon begins, taking on a more serious tone, "it's basically business psychology with a Japanese twist. Whenever you do something for the second time, psychologically believe that it is the first time you are doing it, and employ the perspective of a clean slate to help yourself approach everything fresh. This helps you realize how you can make improvements."

"Oh, sort of the like the beginner's mind concept from class?" I say, understanding the relativity.

"Yes, just like that," Jon affirms, aware that I understand. "And another thing I should say about KaiZen. It is all about small, incremental improvements rather than large innovations. So we define KaiZen Psychology as the science of incremental improvements for the goal of great change."

Now I want to make this relevant to what I already know. "Have you read Thoreau, Emerson, Hawthorne... any of the transcendental literature?"

"Yes, I am well aware," says Jon, humbled.

"How does KaiZen fit into all that?" I second guess myself. "Wait... forget that question, it doesn't."

"No, no," Jon counters, "it relates. You see, whenever we transcend a layer of consciousness, we make a lasting incremental improvement and are forever different; through transcendence we change our world permanently."

I nod, still listening.

Jon continues, "This improvement is permanently stored within the field of our habitual quantum reality. The change we make then becomes an available template for all other beings on a pathway of resonance similar to our own."

I smile; he even tied it into Morph 101 material. I wonder, was he in my class last semester? He is such an ordinary looking person, and blends in so well, I doubt I would have noticed.

"Hmm," I think out loud, "so how would one use KaiZen to write an awesome term paper if they had too much knowledge and evidence for their own good?"

"Well, one would start with the small things, making the best out of what most immediately surrounds them... like picking low-hanging fruit. Do the easy things first, then little by little re-organize what you have into the perfect order, creating the purest form, until, finally, all that remains is pure, perfect, clear information, free for the taking. If you are intelligent enough you will find a way around any obstacle."

"So what you're saying is that if I want to use KaiZen Psychology when writing a paper, I should first organize my quotes, writing up little summaries and the paper will take care of itself?"

"Yeah," Jon acquiesces. "That is one way to do it. So if that is your way, that is your way. Everyday you just do things a little different, a little better. To do that is to KaiZen. But don't just apply it to school work; apply it to something fun like a sport, martial art or relationship."

"Everyday do something a little different, a little better," I parrot. "I like it, I like it." His suggestion to apply it to relationships reminds me of Lauren. "Now tell me something else, Jon. How do you KaiZen your life when a relationship ends?"

"Well, having them in your life, not having them in your life... no difference." He comes back, as if that is a simple answer.

"What? No difference? Jon, that's a big difference!"

"Yeah, if you are living in a world of duality, it's a big difference. But out beyond all ideas of what's good in my life, what's bad in my life, what I want, what I don't want... there's a field. I'll meet you there."

"Damn," I think. "I didn't know I was talking to Rumi."

This guy has some wisdom though. Maybe I can pick his brain for more nuggets.

"So then," I begin, "what is love?"

Inquiring within, he eventually answers: "Love is like enlightenment. As far as I'm concerned, enlightenment is a perpetual state of love... a love so profound that we experience it everywhere we go and in everything we do."

"So basically, for the enlightened one, love overflows from within and knows no bounds?"

"Yeah, kinda," says Jon.

"Each path to enlightenment is unique. Only I know my Way, and as I embrace my Way it can become a new way for others. We all, in one way or another, pioneer our own destiny, leaving a trail behind."

I don't get it. Am I to walk this path alone? Can the Way only be lived on the individual level? What the hell... why do individual paths not permit not co-pilots? This ain't fair, I tell you, this ain't fair.

Chapter Eight
Putting Fear in Place

For weeks I had no idea what Lauren meant when she broke up with me. I am not open with her? What the hell does that mean? Our whole time together I never told her about my gift, my ability, but that it something I only tell few, select individuals anyways. There's got to be something more to this.

One day, while we were meditating in Buddhist Practice, my answer rose to the surface. I realized that all my life I've had this problem of holding back my emotions. I refuse to expose my tender side. The world shall know nothing of my vulnerability!

I want to come across as a tough guy; that is the image I hold of myself. I am invincible to pain and I have no soft emotions. Yeah, world, that's who I am. Read it and weep.

But why would a girl want to see that side of me? What good would it do? I choose not to open myself up to others as a means of protecting myself. It's a defense mechanism. I will not set myself up to get hurt, especially in a relationship.

Why reveal how vulnerable I am? What's the point? I don't get it. I figure that as long as I present myself as psychologically strong, maintaining relationships will be a breeze. But maybe that is not always the case?

If only there was some way I could work through this issue. I feel that the root runs deep. But how deep? What is the source of this? How did I form this fearful habit? And most importantly, what can I do to change it?

Despite what Mr. Manifest said about instantly changing your life with intention, change is hard. It may come easy for him, but for me it's like pulling teeth. I rarely admit this, but I often feel trapped in a cage of negative energy. I become it's victim; I cannot just simply escape the negativity that enshrouds. I don't want it, but I get stuck. What do I do? How do I "think myself" out of this one, Mr. Manifest?

January and February pass. Jon and I became close friends and would often find ourselves in heated conversations about the nature of life and consciousness. He has spent a lot of time at Shambhala centers with Lamas, Rinpoches and meditation-aficionados. He, himself, is a big time meditator, devoting an hour upon waking and an hour before sleeping, or so he claims. I now have the impression that a daily practice of meditation brings one a clarity and insight that cannot be found in any other way. Good for them. But I don't think that is the only path; hence the fire.

It wasn't until March that I figured out how to work through my issues and confront the negativity. I remembered that gift certificate aunt Patty got me for my birthday, to see the hypnotherapist. Now would be the perfect time to use it.

That very day in early March I called, making an appointment during my spring break, as I would be home that week and Sally Bearse's office is in the area.

Deep down, something tells me that this will help me find the root of my opening up problem and the negativity that comes with it. I knew it came for a reason.

Today is the day of my hypnotherapy session with Sally. I arrive 15 minutes early. As Jon would say, "When you're early, you're on time. When you're on time, you're late." I park the car, power down the iPod, remove the keys and exit the vehicle.

As I stand outside my car, preparing to step into the small office building, a warm breeze brushes my face. I pick up on a faint scent of daffodils. Lovely. Spring. New Nature. Can't beat it.

Entering the building, I look on the wall at a listing of offices and find hers. 2B. I go up the stairs, walk down the hall of the second floor, following the signs and come to her door. I take a second to read her specialties listed on the opaque glass.

2B
Sally Bearse
Hypnotherapy · Past Life Regression · Life Between Lives

Walking into the room, I am greeted by gentle, trickling water and flourishing plants of all kinds. There is great energy to this waiting room. If the session doesn't heal me, this room alone will.

As I hang up my jacket she walks out of one of the three rooms on the far wall and motions for me to come in. She must have been expecting me.

The session begins with the typical protocol of background, psychological history and reasons for seeking her services. I briefly explain what happened between Lauren and I, how I have a resistance to being fully open in relationships and how difficult it is for me to battle negative energy.

"Sounds to me like a past life issue," she says, pushing up her glasses as she examines the notes she's been taking.

"What?" I respond, shocked. "You mean past lives actually exist?"

"Yes," she answers confidently.

In disbelief, I insist on more information. "What proof do you have? I am skeptical. How can you make such assumptions?"

She doesn't lose her cool. "Believe it or not, there is actually a science to it. And being the young and aspiring Quantum PsychoPhysicist that you are, I think you will find this quite interesting. The field of work I do is based on thousands upon thousands of case studies in which we hypnotherapists bring clients into an omniscient, trance-like state where they may become aware of past lives. Anything and everything that happened to them, what they did, what they hoped to achieve in that lifetime and what they wish they had done differently at the end of it all... all that information returns to the surface."

"But wait," I say, trying to fill in the gaps. "If we have access to all of that information, how come we do not already know this? Why would we go about living human lives under the impression that this here life is our only shot if it really isn't?"

"Because," she reasons, "if we did not come into this world a blank-slate, we would get so hung up on recurring patterns and mistakes that we would further distract ourselves from our present life and how we want it to be different. By not knowing, we stay more present."

"So if this information isn't in our immediate memory, where is it?"

"We come in with prior knowledge of a specific mission, but it is all subconscious. If we repeat a pattern in this life, the subconscious wants us to look at it and will call our attention. The reason is because we are to discover our mission along the way. Life's all about the mystery."

"But *I* am hung up. What do I do?"

"Relax. It's just stuck energy. Just learn from it and let it go."

"Oh, alright," I respond, beginning to open my mind to the idea and trying to understand how all this past-life-stuck-energy present-life-interference works. "It's for the best that we do not have a full memory of past lives. I get it. And your field of therapy works by reminding us of the most important issues we have had so that we can deal with them in our present lifetimes, so we can get out of our rut?"

"Yes," says Sally. "It is all a process of letting go and forgiving so that we ourselves may evolve. And that is exactly what my work does... It will bring you to the root of your opening up problem. Like I said, it sounds serious; it is probably a past life habit. Today we will find out where it comes from and from what lifetime. It is clearly a strong force that is getting in your way, but we will move through this obstacle, together."

"Great," I say. "I can't wait to get started. But the scientist in me is curious. Tell me a bit about these case studies you mentioned."

"Sure," says Sally, happy to share. "Michael Newton, a master hypnotherapist, has written several books on the Spirit World. That is where we return to between lives. And it is really not that hard to understand if you look at the parallels structured within our universe. It's all as a metaphor, or a micro of the macro. According to

Newton's research, Earth is just another school. No matter what career we choose or what we end up doing, all we are here to do is learn. We are on Earth for some sort of spiritual education, to mature as souls in a universe of thousands and thousands of life-bearing celestial bodies as we prepare to graduate to the more advanced planets. That is simply what Earth life is about."

"And he even goes into detail on these other planets," she continues. "Through his research we now know that there are places where sentient beings, much similar to ourselves, create trees and rocks with thought, give birth to stars, travel at light speed from place to place... things we only think real in sci-fi films. But the older souls here on Earth have lived on those planets and done that before... we are not alone."

Chapter Nine
Oem: the Man, the Myth, the Legend

We are deep in the heart of the therapy session. My body is as relaxed as it is while sleeping, but I still have an awareness of myself. That is the difference; It's like falling asleep but without really falling. One remains conscious.

We are exploring my most immediate past life, as a man named Oem who lived during the 1920s.

"Now tell me," Sally prods, "as Oem, what did you do?"

Although in a trance, I can still hear her voice. Gazing into this former life, I describe the pictures I see within. "I was an inventor, a visionary, a pioneer... this is so cool! I can see it so clearly... all the positive energy always flowing through me, invigorating me day in and day out."

"You seem very excited about the work you did."

"Yes," I confirm. "It was my calling. I found it in that life and gave it my all."

"Good, good. Now, what else can you tell me about this life, did you have a family?"

I now look into a different part of that life experience. There is much more. "Yes, I did. A beautiful wife. Her name was Ros Well. Wow, I remember her now, the aura about her, the way we interacted. She made me feel so special. Whenever I was around her it brought this sacred energy out of me, I felt so light hearted and on top of the world when we would spend time together. We did also had some children, but that is fuzzy."

"She probably helped you maintain your positive attitude and creative flow while brainstorming and inventing."

I look deeper into our relationship. "Yes, she helped me through many emotional struggles. She was so willing to help, always at my side, believing in my aspirations, it was perfect for what I needed then."

"What else can you tell me about her? What else do you feel?"

I become aware of the not-so-happy parts of that life.

"I also feel some clouds."

"Clouds?"

"Yeah, like a hovering negativity."

We've struck oil! Sally wants to learn more. "Go on."

"Well, I'm starting to see how I spent more time on my inventions and self-improvement than on quality time with her and the children. Way more time than I should have. I would often not go to bed until 2 or 3 am, sleep in while everyone went off to work and school and only really interact with the family around dinner time. But it wasn't like that all the time. At night we would sometimes gather in the living room and read to each other, talk about our day or listen to the radio."

"So you didn't completely ignore them," she says, getting a balanced picture.

"No, not completely. But the balance between time I spent on myself and time I spent on my family was certainly not equal." I now feel an intense feeling of regret. Tears begin to drip from my eyes as I realize the sheer beauty of what I once had and how much better it could have been, had I been more social and open to my family.

I have a clear image of Ros Well in my mind now. "God, she was so beautiful, I can't believe all the great opportunities I missed on, all the extra love we could of shared. She died not knowing that I truly loved her, and now it's gone, all gone!" I have become so disturbed by this negative energy that I awaken from the trance, in tears.

I'm sure this is nothing new for Sally, as there is a box of tissues right by the futon I've been sprawled out on.

"Relax," says Sally, calmly bringing me back to the present. "You have to release this energy. Life on Earth is all about learning. Listen to me, just as you reincarnated, so has she. Soulmates have a way of finding each other again, don't worry. The odds of crossing paths are one in a million, but the spiritual that force binds two souls together is stronger than any obstacle."

"Oh, I see," I chime in, feeling a little relieved.

She continues to console me. "You are a college freshman; most of my clients are in their 40s and 50s. You have the rest of your life ahead of you. Just enjoy the little things right now. Everything will be fine. The most important thing is that you now have the knowledge that will get you through it."

"But what about the negativity, how do I deal with that?"

"We all have different ways to deal with negative energy," Sally reasons. "But now that you know where this fear of yours comes from, use the knowledge to set you free."

I spent the rest of that day thinking about the knowledge I had gained of my past. I neglected a perfect family, and now I struggle to again be open in a relationship.

When I fear this, I invite negativity in my life. But, if I challenge the fear, and freely expose myself to the world, will that expel the negativity? Will that diffuse the light patterns holding me back?

I remember what Dr. Rupert had told us the last time we saw him, when Lauren and I turned in our term papers. *Sustain the best resonance, any way possible and by any means necessary.* The only obstacle I see to my highest resonance is this fear of being open. If I overcome this, what could stand in my way?

Essentially, what I learned today is that my last incarnation was that of a very accomplished, determined man, Oem, who would stop at nothing to improve himself and find enlightenment through various attempts and inventions. Aside from working on creations and testing hypothesis' late into the night, he had spent many hours in meditation and in contemplation, reading the wise words of ancient ones.

Little did Oem know, though, that enlightenment was right before his very eyes, in his own bed every night with his true lover, Ros Well. The easiest, most direct path to enlightenment was overlooked. Sadly, he died a man with a strong mind but a weak heart.

But, this past will not burden me. I am me, I am not Oem. Here I am, living again, as a new person. Enlightenment lies within the heart; why seek it elsewhere?

Chapter Ten
The Quest Begins

I return to school from spring break feeling renewed; probably the combination of a week without worries of homework, exams and deadlines, the new path of virtue I made for ex-wrestler Diamond Dallas Page, and the insight that came from my hypnotherapy session.

What new path for DDP, you ask? Well, according to every TV news station, he had a midlife crisis, hit rock bottom and wound-up in an intensive care rehab center. Him being my favorite wrestler, I couldn't just sit back and let this happen. So, I brought us into a world where rather than entering the post-partum depression of our beloved WCW ceasing to be, Diamond Dallas Page embraced this change in professional entertainment and became a yoga guru, imparting pearls of wisdom to the public through asana as a celebrity who really made something of himself.

But back to the insight of my session with Sally Bearse. I finally know the source of my fear. I now know what Lauren meant about me being "closed" and why she broke up with me. I can be who she wants me to be now. I wonder if she will take me back?

Wait... why would I want to be with someone who can't love and accept me for who I am, who can't stick it out with me as I grow into a better person and learn to open up? Aren't relationships all about growing together, learning new things, becoming new people and experiencing the world side-by-side?

Recalling my past life, I superimpose that over my current situation. If Lauren had true feelings for me, the way Ros Well did for Oem, why didn't she stay with me? Yeah, I am timid, I'm not completely open, but so what? I wanted to work through it, but she didn't; she just gave up. *And* she's with Chad now. It hurts.

But oh well. What more could I have done? I was willing to make adjustments and try to make it work, she wasn't, so that's the end of that. I guess that's what you get for dating the good-looking, popular chick in class.

On my way to class I cue up my iPod. This is a daily thing for me; I've come to know recorded music as a quantum tool. And for certain songs, I just can't get enough. I'm addicted to the transformation like hooked on phonics.

Every time we listen to a track we are exposed to the same moment in history when those resonances were captured, and the more we listen to it, and love what we are hearing, the greater that moment becomes for the people in the studio. Time is but a permeable surface; all aspects of it are highly influential.

Pressing the bottom button of the click wheel, A song starts playing that I have never heard before. I can tell it is by Angels & Airwaves, that much is certain, but for some reason, where it should say album title, all it says is *Soon to be released*. There is no artwork, either. This is interesting, because I've been listening to AVA non-stop since I got this baby and I *know* this track has not been on here before today. Perhaps this is what Tom meant by it being a "magic iPod"? New songs just magically appear?

It does give a title though. Apparently this song is called *Shove*. I jam out to the chill beat, listening closely to the lyrics:

Forget the things that you own,
And travel almost any where you can go...
   (Shove)

There's something strange about this musical device. I feel like it always gives me the exact message I need to hear through the music it shuffles to the surface. I think about the Shove lyrics, wondering how it might relate to my current situation.

Recently I learned that the root of my difficulty, my trouble of being open in relationships, comes from that past life with Ros Well. I did not give her as much attention as I should have, and that left me with this spiritual scar, this fear, this inability to fully open up to a significant other.

Forgetting the things I own will not be a problem, but where should I go? Should I go off in search of Ros Well reincarnate and apologize?

No, that wouldn't work. How would she even know who I am? It would probably just be really creepy and super-awkward.

But even if I did try to do that, how would I find her? I want to find her, I have an interest in seeing her again. Part of me feels that I will never resolve this fear within until we reunite, until I can let her know how I truly feel and start fresh with her this time around. But how does one go about this? Am I rushing things? I don't know what to do, I really don't.

I know I have the rest of my life to find her, but I cannot ignore this inner impatience. I want to make it up to her, and I want to do it now. And considering the message I just got, if my iPod is as "magical" as Tom claims, I should just leave everything here, forget it all, and travel in search of her. Maybe this is "the next adventure" I was asked about being ready for, the message

I wrote down in my Morph 101 notebook the first day of school last September.

I'm walking to class, but taking the long way, the scenic route, giving myself some time to reflect. Something happened when I relived those memories in Sally's office. Some internal shift. Some sort of existential validation. During that session I felt so connected, so in love, just as Jon had described... the perpetual state of true love. I now understand it because I have felt it on a personal level. But rather than finding it by myself, I found it with another.

The entire day has gone by and it is now nighttime. I lay here in bed, listening to Angels & Airwaves, and I can't help but reminisce on the past life experiences I had with Ros Well~ all the memories that hypnotherapy session conjured up for me.

Just thinking about her, and those precious memories we shared... God, I love her. I truely do. I remember the sweet nature-y smell to her hair, like a blend of acorns and autumn leaves, the glow in her hazel eyes like the most beautiful star in the night time sky.

How I long to be with her now, whoever she is or wherever she has chosen to incarnate. To embrace that soul once more, to feel her heart beating against mine, to hold her hand as our bodily pulses ebb and flow, back and forth within each other...

Is this why I feel a hollowness? Will my fear never resolve until the day we meet? I'm afraid that without her I can never be completely whole. She is my other half, my eternal significant other, the one I was once divided from and am now destined to rejoin.

Yeah, *Shove* was on to something. I will begin this quest, to find again my true love~ to expose my tender heart in a way more genuine than I ever have before~ to offer myself completely, to let her know that in this life, this time around, I will not repeat the mistakes of Oem.

I take my headphones off to surround myself in silence. I lay here in bed, realizing how much Ros Well meant to Oem and how just having her in my life again will do something for me that no one else can do.

Only she can heal my wound, only she can provide the love that will dissolve my fear permanently. Only through her can I learn the true meaning of life, which is to love it, and the true meaning of love, which is to live it.

Have you ever heard
A sad heart buried alive?
You can do almost anything.
    (Call to Arms)

Just like the first day, these whispers come to my awareness. But this time I recognize it. Those are the exact same words from an Angels & Airwaves song. But how is this music whispering itself into my head? And why?

Sometimes I think in music. Or maybe, the music is thinking through me.

On this temperate winter night I peer out the window through the trees and the street lights beyond them.

The lights they peer out
of the leafless trees
And you won't be alone,
I am beside you.
   (True Love)

More whispers. So mysterious, yet so fitting... exactly what I was doing, and exactly what I need: someone beside me. I am the music, in part. But who is the one beside me? What is this... internal music communication... all about?

Sally did say that our guardian angels and spirit guides attempt to communicate with us through music, planting tunes in our heads at key times throughout our life as a way for us to get certain messages and inspire us to take certain actions. Whether or not we are listening and receptive to them is our own choice.

Listen, we are never alone. There is always something, some guiding force, at our side helping us make decisions, navigate this chaotic world, watching over us. Some close themselves off to this guidance, but it is always there. And this research Sally mentioned, that of

Michael Newton, gives evidence to the fact that we do have guardian angels with us in this world, as part of our existence.

The question then becomes, what is my guide trying to tell me? Does he want me to leave school? Is he trying to help me find my soulmate again? God, I will take any help I can get. I want to fill this hollowness.

I continue laying here in bed, exhausted from a the long day of classes, homework and gym time. Since I learned of Ros Well, there's been an unbreakable pattern. At the end of the day it all comes back to thoughts of her... it all comes back to that longing to fill the void, to be with her once again and set everything right.

And I wonder, does she yearn for me just as I yearn for her? How does she feel? Is she even aware of my presence? Does she at all care?

I toss in bed with a head full of questions and a heart full of sadness. I am sad because now that I know she is out there, I miss her. I am eager to share this life with her. All I can think about is how this time around I will do things differently.

What we have is a true form of love. Since the dawn of our soul we have been destined to live out eternity together. All soulmates were actually once one soul, until the universe thought it would be fun to have souls divide themselves and play the game of finding each other time and time again. But that makes sense. Through play, we discover the universe. This is just the universe's way of getting us to truly know it.

> *I cannot live,*
> *I cannot breathe*
> *Unless you do this with me.*
> *(The Adventure)*

Finding her is all about playing the game of life. But until that point, I will never really be complete. I will never truly know peace until I am with her again and in her presence. People strive for enlightenment, to better their own self, but what about bettering the self that is the selfless one living through someone else?

I think much of the presence Buddhism has in today's society, and how it affects people like Jon. He is so dead-set on "finding enlightenment" that he often withdraws from social situations just so he can have more time to meditate and improve himself.

Meditation is great, and so is self-improvement, but you have to have balance in your life. You don't need to be perfect to have fun with friends and enjoy the world. Bettering one's self is important, but interacting with others and sharing your unique energy and perspective on things is just as important. No amount of meditation will ever change one's true nature; we must exchange who we are. By sharing resonance we evolve the universe.

So many people get lost in the quest for personal enlightenment. They completely neglect the quest for romantic enlightenment, a kind of interpersonal enlightenment, a true love experienced between two hearts as it evolves the consciousness of both involved. The journey, and the romantic journey, is so beautiful, and the addition of another to share these experiences makes it that much sweeter.

I power-down my mind for the night with the thought that I cannot live the life I'm destined to without her by my side. Just as *The Adventure* goes, I need her to do this with me.

I make one final effort to put my mind at rest and fall asleep. I put the headphones back on and press play.

Oh I need you now,
The Earth fell fast asleep.
This room is safe and sound,
will you lay here with me?
(Good Day)

Thoughts fade into feelings, feelings of what it will be like when we first meet. The world will be reborn... everything will feel new, refreshed, super-charged. I faintly remember what it was like spending my life with her last time. I can remember the feeling of her energy... so pure, open, loving, light-hearted... so perfect. Feeling this soothes my restless mind. One day we shall be reunited. It is written in the stars.

I drift off into delta, entering a deep sleep. My body is calm, my mind subdued ~ tranquil ~ hopeful. As I enter that sleep state where we lose consciousness, when we let go of our ourselves like a fisherman cutting the line to a fish he caught but no longer desires, I listen to the angelic music of Tom DeLonge and company on my iPod. It helps me dream pleasantly. It is an inner cosmic solace.

I become aware of nothing at all. For this moment I do not exist. Nothing exists. I even perceive not the music I have playing to my ears in the physical world. Even though I return to this place every time before dreaming, it still feels so mysterious, and somewhat magical. I could imagine that this is what the universe was like before the big bang. Without form and void.

Yet, from this darkness comes a faint light in the distance. I become slightly aware of my self, of the ego that is my shell, my container, that makes me an entity unique from everything else.

A voice softly call to me. "Hey, hey you! It's Tom, Thomas DeLonge, your guardian angel. I want to show you something, take you somewhere."

"What?" I think in response, unaware that I am communicating telepathically. "How can you be an angel if you are a living person?"

"Well it's a long story, but if you must ask..." he takes a moment to cultivate a thoughtful explanation. "Basically, after launching into deep space in 2006 I found planet Heaven. I was drawn into it. And there I transfigured; my body became a body of light. I transformed into the ethereal form you know and see me as now.

"And there is something very special about you. The fate of Earth depends on it, on you. You may not know or understand this now, but one day you will. And I know everything you are going through, with your aching heart and desire to be with your soulmate once more. This is why I have come to you tonight. I actually visit you every night before you dream just to plant silly things in your subconscious, or tell you of all the travels I've done here in space with the freedom of the light body, all the different alien races I have met. I live a real Star Trek, but better.

"But, the reason I come to you tonight is because I want to remind you of her, of a precious memory you two shared, of a life when things were perfectly balanced. It is time for you to get another taste of her so that you can shift your focus to more important things. You have the rest of your life to find her; true love is something one cannot rush. So, let yourself do what you normally do. Relax and let yourself dream. I will be here with you the whole time, you will be safe.

"I will guide your dream," Tom continues. "I will help you find her again for this one night. Just pay attention. When you meet her tonight, recognize her energetic signature... there is nothing else in the universe like it. I can't tell you where or who she is now, but pay attention for the clues and the hints from this night forward and you will find her as I guide you."

The light becomes brighter, iridescent and louder. I look into it. I melt.

A star, bright and loud,
is in dire need
And that fear,
it is an empty fear inside you.
(True Love)

The light engulfs me. I become aware again of being in a body, only it has much less weight; it is a dream-body. Everything feels so subtle and refined, tangible yet intangible.

The next thing I know, I am in a forest, walking. I have a sense that I'm walking to meet someone. Wait, it's her. It's her! I can feel her presence, her energy extending out through this entire forest. Her amber aura projects like sunlight reaching for the moon.

I tune into her energy. I can almost feel her. This is what it will be like to find her again, I just know it. The energy will call me; it will draw me in. I make a mental note of this feeling. God, angels know just what to give us.

I look down to take inventory. I am wearing hand-made brown clothes, probably of some animal skin. I am also barefoot. Judging by the fleshiness of my smooth hairless feet, I'd say I'm no older than 12 or 13.

I walk forth. I go up a hill. The sound of rushing water greets me. A hundred yards up, I come to a river. Following the flow of water upstream, I ascend a mountain side. Narrowly outstretching both arms, I wedge myself through thickets of young trees.

A dreamlike musical soundscape washes over the land, something that can only happen at times like this. The best way I can describe this would be a cross between *Stars of Bethlehem* and the beginning of *Valkyrie Missile*. If Tom always does this in my dreams, I should awaken to my dreams more often.

The feeling of her energy gets stronger and stronger as I graduate from the thickets to a large open space. I see a beautiful pool of water beneath a gorgeous thirty foot waterfall, all surrounded by rocks in the near distance.

Atop the waterfall she stands, patient as a bird on the ledge of a building, as if waiting for me. My heartbeat quickens in anticipation. She has been expecting me. I get a sense that in this lifetime we met here often; it was one of our spots. But this particular time feels like the first. First time, best time.

The closer I get, the more majestic the music ignites and resounds, making the entire experience divine. No doubt Tom is with me, composing music in some highly advanced, angelic way of universal expression, setting the tone for this dream that is but a recollection of a blissful spiritual memory.

Think of what it would sound like to blend *The Adventure*, *Good Day* and *The Gift*, with a dash of *True Love*. That is how awesome this live, ethereal music sounds right now. This dream is a movie and he is the film scorer. The instant he thinks of an idea for the music, it reverberates; with the very thought, it becomes so. That is just one thing that angels such as he are capable of. They create highly intricate airwaves at will. And it is so perfect just the way it is, for this is how angels do. Spontaneous perfection.

I walk closer to the waterfall. She acknowledges my presence and smiles, glowing from within. Sun breaks through leaves and highlights her natural blond hair. She is now even more radiant. Enzymes of happiness flood my mouth. Love is in the air.

I walk to the top of the hill where the waterfall begins. She thrusts out her arms, awaiting my embrace with gusto. Enchanted by her deep blue eyes, I run into the embrace as if I had not seen her for a hundred years.

This feeling of resonating with her energy once more is indescribable. In this moment I am complete. I am bliss. No, *we* are bliss.

Tom continues to set the mood with his divine orchestration. So out of this world. As I pull her in closer, hugging tighter, the music intensifies. He knows what is going to happen before I do it. All I really have to do is follow the music.

We all are love
And love is hard,
So here's my heart.
    (Some Origins of Fire)

The bliss I feel right now in this embrace with her is unparalleled. This is the completeness I seek. I find it with her. Nothing else can make me feel this way.

She pulls her head back, tilts to her right shoulder and leans in halfway for a kiss. I lean in, meeting her halfway. We kiss with the energy of a first time. Perhaps, in this lifetime, it was. I feel so charged, so empowered, so alive!

There is something to be said for this magical feeling, for the empowerment that comes with a moment such as this. With this kiss, a new world was born. We become the masculine and feminine forces of the universe, like the entire world revolves around our divine will. We teenagers are the creators, at least in our own little world.

We are infinite energy. We are the boundlessness of the cosmos that cannot be contained. We are the essence of all that is and could ever be. Man and woman, separate, yet inseparable. Here, yet everywhere.

Her lips melt into mine as her sweet saliva drips onto my tongue. These enzymes are loaded with endorphins and I cannot get enough of them. This is it.

This is the feeling of love. And not just any love. It is *her* love, *our* love. Could any feeling of enlightenment ever top this?

> *The cure is if you let in*
> *just a little more love.*
> *I promise you this,*
> *a little's enough.*
>
> (A Little's Enough)

Tom is right. The love I receive from her is my cure. It is my elixir. I let in her love. It saturates me to the core. This is the greatest medicine anyone could ever conceive of. Love. Just love. And it is just that simple.

This kiss slowly ends and we both open our eyes, faces less than an inch away from each other. I peer into those deep blue eyes as she does into mine. I see the world, I see galaxies, I see a never ending fractal, an infinite expansion.

We stand here, embraced, eyes locked for hours. We don't speak a word; we don't need to. The energy that precedes thought flows between us and speaks on our behalf. Energetically, we had the greatest, most beautiful conversation without a single utterance. With this live divine music and song from Tom DeLonge, who needs words?

The sun starts to set and we break our gaze to look at it. We peer off to the right, watching it set beneath trees. The sky is full of pinks and reds as the burning orange ball descends.

Never has a sunset been more breath-taking than now, as if all the beauty of the world heightens when you're in love. It all becomes richer. The music softens as does the sky.

From another part of the sky, a pale moon rises. Then a bright star. Then other bright stars. I look back at her.

> *The stars in your eyes light up the sky*
> *with thoughts, light and fire and sound*
> **Imagine, Imagine**
> *(Love Like Rockets)*

A little twinkle in her eye glistens as a jewel encrusted sky of lights reflect from her pupils. A calm comes over me and I start to hear Tom's voice again, bringing me out of the dream. "Hey, you know who else loved her the way you did?"

"Who?" I ask, confused he would ask such a random question and kill the perfect mood.

"Your Dad."

Tom, always a kidder with the Dad jokes, even as an angel.

"But seriously, remember how you feel with her now. Remember this energy. This is how you will recognize her again in the future."

I try to explain it to him. "It feels unique... I have never felt anything else like this, any other kind of love, of this magnitude..."

"That is because she is your soulmate and together you amplify each other with unconditional love. It has a special power because of the spiritual history behind it; the fate that binds you two together throughout time brings a quality to it that is unparalleled.

"So remember what this feels like, because this will help you find her again. Now, that is all I can say for tonight. I have done my job. When you wake up, your iPod will have a brand new album on it. *LOVE*. Whenever you need help finding or remembering her, I want you to listen to this. It will guide your way. *LOVE* is the resonance of the romantic enlightenment you seek.

"Also, if you wouldn't mind, send the MP3s over to my modlife buddies so they can upload it to the site. And tell them to set it up as a free album download; that way everyone can get it. You are really the only way I have to get my music distributed on Earth now. I am an angel, I can make miracles, but for these human tasks I need your help."

"No problem at all," I comply. "Will it sound like the music I heard in this dream?"

"Yes, and then some!" says Tom. "And there is one more very important thing I must tell you. Earth time for you right now is still early 2011, but come 2012, near the end of that year, something will happen that requires your attention. Your full attention. There will be a . . . "

My roommate's alarm clock blazes, instantly pulling me from the dreamworld. Damnit! What was Tom saying? 2012? Like the movie? Like the money-hungry ad I saw near the stairwell? Is that really going to happen?

And what does that have to do with me? I'm just an aspiring Quantum PsychoPhysicist... I'm no geologist; I'm no astronomer. What could *I* can do?

Awakening fully from my dream state, I become conscious again of the lack of her in my life. That dream brought back feelings of her. It brought back an energy I have long forgotten... the energy of true love.

Yet, even though we are apart, I feel some sort of connection to her. A connection that doesn't come from the outside... no, it starts from within. When I dive into myself, I find her there. Inside I am reminded of her, and this then amplifies by the fire of her energy when I am in her presence~ so warm, so passionate.

Chapter Eleven
Wish, Dream, Remember

I went about my day with a lighter mood than usual. Last night's dream put me in place. My mind would not stop dwelling on the lack of true love in my life. I was getting sick of my emo-self. You probably were, too.

I remember the feeling of her energy, and now that I know it, I can never forget it. That, and that alone, will pull me through. Having now established a connection within, and having all the romantic resonances of LOVE to remind me, how could I ever feel alone again?

It is now another night. I stand here beneath the evening sky, still all warm and fuzzy from that reconnection twenty-one hours ago. But I wonder, was that dream last night real?

Awake and in this real world, I have my doubts. Tom DeLonge, my personal guardian angel? Yeah, right. What am I thinking? That's crazy. I'm not one to support the pharmaceutical monopoly, but maybe I need help. Well, I guess that's what happens when you fall asleep with your iPod on, streaming your "awesome AVA" playlist subconsciously into the wee hours of the night. It was all in my head.

Let's do as would Jon, and enter the pure. I transcend thought, attend to the Now, listening to my environment. My favorite star once more draws me in. A delicate calm suddenly comes over me, standing under these stars and feeling that one star in particular. This twilight and it's accompanying solitude puts me at ease. My troubles melt away like a snow flake passing through a summer's breeze.

Sustaining my connection to her, I wonder where she is, how her life is unfolding, and whether or not she feels the way I do. This feeling of love is different than what I felt with Lauren; this love is grounded. I thought Lauren and I had something solid, but since our break-up I've realized that what we had was just young love, a lust-kinda thing, different than true love.

I remember what Sally said about soulmates being mysteriously drawn together. What is this spiritual force that binds us? How do soulmates gravity to each other, always finding a way that works, like branches in a forest diverting towards light?

> *It can be so bold and so cavalier,*
> *To reach out to the fire her soul's sending here.*
> *(Shove)*

If she reaches out for me, I will reach out for her. A separation of physical distance is only a separation in one's mind. When two hearts form one destiny, obstacles are just figments of the imagination. Finding each other again is but the game of life, the new exploration, a reprisal of one's eternal identity as validated by one's other half.

Tonight there is no moon in the sky, but that is okay. The stars are what I'm really out here for, anyways. This is a perfect time to wish, to make my intentions clear, before the entire universe above.

> *If you wish it, wish it now.*
> *If you wish it, wish it loud.*
> *If you want it, say it now.*
> *If you want it, say it loud!*
> *We all make mistakes,*
> *Here's your lifeline...*
>
> *(Lifeline)*

My favorite star shines brighter, as if in anticipation. "I wish to learn to love again, to be with you! I wish to redeem myself and love undividedly!" I wish loudly into this one star above, hoping she hears me, wherever she is. Somewhere out there, this same star that I see is visible to her, too.

Love Beyond Life

May the truth that connects us carry my wish.

A few feet away, a ball of light, something like a hologram, materializes in human form. With this form comes music. I can hardly make out the details, but the more I look, the less I believe. It's Tom! Could it be, Tom DeLonge, my guardian, for real? Pinch me now. PINCH ME NOW

"Well hello there!" He says in an ever so welcoming and friendly voice as he coasts over toward me. "You're making it real, transcending the barrier between day life and night life. Do you know why our bodies are programmed to sleep at night rather than during the day?"

"It's calmer?" I guess.

"Yeah," Tom replies, "But what makes it calmer?"

Perhaps the answer is in my environment. "These stars, the delicate light poking through the darkness, yes?"

"Very good," Tom sanctions. "And when we dream, that is just as real as any day life experience, only it is our chance to create the day as we would will it. The ball is in our court. At night, we become the creative centers of our world. During day, we live a world that has already been created for us.

"And that is the balance between man and God. We are both the creators, and technically we are all God, as a divine spark animates all life, but the acting God-force that appears as more powerful than ourselves has set things up so that during the day we are subject to His will, and during the night, He to our will. We are in a constant teaching/learning relationship with our creator. Awake, we experience Him. Asleep, He experiences us."

I wonder what Tom is getting at. "So you're saying that I'm not the only one creating reality?"

"Well, you are not, because each dream is a created reality, and we all dream, but you have refined this skill to a level higher than most people. That is why we need your help as 2012 approaches."

Again with the 2012 thing. Instantly, this reference triggers a memory of the end of my dream. He was beginning to warn me about something right before I woke up. So I guess last night was real.

Yet still I doubt. "What do you mean? What could *I* do?"

"Don't worry, you will see, we still have a year to go. And in that year I will train and prepare you."

Now I have *no* idea what is going on. "Prepare me... for what?"

"The end of the world!" Tom replies, sarcastically frustrated. "What do you think?!"

"Alright. Fine," I cave, not fully cognizant of the responsibility I'm assuming. "Just tell me what I must do to prepare."

"You must outgrow your attachment."

"Huh? What attachment?" I respond, confused.

"The one to your soulmate."

My energy plummets. "But, but..." I'm struggling, resisting the request. I employ *Adventure* lyrics with an interpretive twist: "without her I cannot live, without her I will never know true love and the enlightenment that follows."

"Exactly," Tom says as *Valkyrie Missile* airwaves flood our surroundings. Everything becomes divine. "You had one wish for something new. And you made that wish, to learn to love again. It is a great wish, and it will be granted, but you first must learn to be whole without her.

Just as the monk detaches from the desire for enlightenment to become enlightened, you must detach from the idea of true love to actually find it. Be yourself; let the love come to you."

I am confused. Everything I've ever received in life has come as a result of effort. He looks at me and closes his eyes, suggesting I tune into the music emanating for me. I listen.

The sounds gracefully build from organs and august-rushes to a simple guitar melody with periodic drum snaps. The vocals kick in, more meaningful than ever. A deeper message backs this music. These sounds are carrier waves of consciousness. I think I am starting to get it.

Last night I had that one experience with her. In that dream of a memory, we embraced for hours and truly felt one another. That has carried me through the entire day. But, that was a gift~ a taste of things to come. For now, it is time to say goodbye. It is time I cultivate my true self, time I obtain an awareness of the true nature of my mind.

~ This is energy ~

~ Who would have thought it would turn out this way?

~ This is the closest thing to emission right now ~

(Valkyrie Missile)

"Listen," Tom reasons, "I know you love her and want her back. All of us angels want that to happen. And it will. Just realize that reunion is a very delicate process with several steps to be taken along the way… steps that are to be taken in full, one at a time. You both have to be ready for each other first. A lot happened in that last life. You neglected her, and she was too lenient, never speaking up about your self-absorption."

The truth hurts, but it's all clear. "I gotcha Tom. I understand."

"Now what you need is strength, inner strength. And not only inner strength, but sound judgment. You must know when to use your ability and when not to. No more cultivating women into your life. You've had your fun. For the next year and a half we need to work with you, and having a romantic relationship will just get in the way."

"I can't even wish in my soulmate?" I come back, disappointed.

"As your guardian angel, I wouldn't recommend it."

I agree to his terms, but need a confirmation. "So, you're saying it wouldn't be wise to wish her into reality?"

"Right, because it is destined to happen anyway," Tom reasons. "True love will only happen naturally; it is God's creation, not yours. You cannot control it."

Now I know why he started off with that lecture on dream-worlds versus real-worlds. I understand completely.

Thus began the truth of the quest.

Chapter Twelve
The Quest Continues

Having come back inside, I lay here in bed with hands crossed behind my head, looking up to the ceiling. I reflect on the conversation Tom and I just had. He is right; it is time I outgrow my attachment. I was figuring this out anyways, but hearing it from the outside makes it that much more important. She is out there, I can feel her, and that will hold me over as I embark on this journey of own, as I realize my Personal Legend.

A wave of satisfaction washes over me, knowing that one day we will be reunited. I cannot help but smile. I anticipate the future.

My thoughts return to what Tom said earlier about becoming independent, finding wholeness first within myself, then sharing that wholeness with another. The way of true love: learning the true nature of your mind and then sharing it with someone else, someone who will bring things out of you that you didn't even know were there.

I suppose that that is the lesson of real love, and it is a love that shines brightly, radiating beyond life. I don't know exactly what happens before or after these human lives, aside from the spiritual immortality research of Michael Newton, but for some strange reason I have a strong feeling that the love I feel now will always be here, regardless of the life. It is simply too strong of an energy to not exist.

Could it be, then, that we live to exchange love? At the end of life do we come to the realization that all we were here to do was give love? Receive love? Cherish it? Basque in it?

Love Beyond Life

Long ago, an old friend told me that love makes the world go round. I didn't believe her then, but now I do. Now I get it. We are driven by emotion and a desire to perpetually be in a perfect state of love. It is as if we are always working to experience this love in any way, shape or form possible. Could this be a universal human quest?

Tom's idea of independence makes perfect sense. The trick to successfully living this human life is learning how to first find the love we seek within. I think that's what he's trying to get through to me.

Women come and go... I cannot rely on them as my main source of love. They are a source, and a powerful one at that, but I first must connect to the love source within if I am to truly appreciate the love sent to me from another.

Just as I complete that thought in my head, a streak of light fills my room. It is twilight; must be 2 or 3 am. All is quiet, and here comes a mysterious ray of light through the window.

It is too bright to be from a car, and also, judging by the angle, it is sourced much higher than the ground.

With this light comes a feeling of peacefulness, a feeling inexplicable.

I do not understand it. What is this? Where is it coming from? And why does it make me feel so safe, so connected?

I get out of bed to look out the window. This light is coming from high in the sky. I source the exact location in relation to other constellations I already know. This beam is of that star... the one that always has my attention...

Falling into a higher resonance, my left hand raises itself to touch the light. The star beams into my hand. It even has a pulsation.

My hand tingles. It's temperature rises by four or five degrees. It feels so toasty.

A sensation of warmth travels up my arm and through my shoulder, finding its way down to my ticker. The light pulses through my body, in sync with the beating of my heart. I have felt this before. I know this feeling. Wow! Yes, this is it!

Sunlight now fills the room. I must have fallen asleep at some point.

Checking my phone for time, as I usually do upon waking, I see I have a text from Lauren, of all people. Funny that I didn't hear it come in. But Lauren? What could she want?

Two months have passed since our break up, in which time she has completely cut me out of her life. No calls, no apologizes, no further explanations, no closure. Curious, though, I open the message.

Hey... we need to talk, call me later. K?

Call her? Why? We need to talk? Um... doesn't she realize that once you break up with someone, you cannot break up with them a second time?

After all she put me through, making me feel like I wasn't good enough for her, not accepting me for who I am and not talking to me for months since our break up... *Now* she wants to talk? A critical period follows the end of relationships, where things can be mended and forgotten, but she is six weeks late. As Mikey said in TMNT I: *Time's up, three bucks off.*

On second thought, I shouldn't be *that* stubborn about it. We did have a great time together last semester. I will hear her out, but not until later on today. I have more important things to do right now, like share myself with people who actually appreciate me.

The day passed like any other. Shower, breakfast, *Kamen Rider*, class, homework, gym, dinner with friends and *Seinfeld*. I missed Seinfeld so much that I had to make Larry David do a reunion episode through *Curb Your Enthusiasm*, and I loved what they did, but nothing beats the originals. And after all that, I decide to give her a call.

She picks up on the first ring. "Hey you!" in a nostalgic tone of voice, as if the cowardly handling of our break up somehow never occurred.

"Hi," I respond after a second, nonchalantly. "What do you wanna talk about?" I say, getting down to business.

"Well," she drags her voice. "I've been thinking... about us..."

"Us?" I snap. "There is no us after you ripped out my heart and stomped all over it, after you refused to talk to me like a real girl about our relationship, after you left me all by myself to figure out what really happened. What, do you think I've just forgotten about that?"

"Listen," she says, trying to get around my tight D. "I know we didn't end on good terms... but like, I was confused. I like, didn't know who I had feelings for, you or Chad, so I thought it would be best to just like, break up with you so I wouldn't end up cheating on you," she admits, desperate for respect and compassion.

"Well why didn't you just tell me that in the first place? You lost feelings for me and developed feelings for someone else. I would have understood that. That happens all the time in high school; I've been there." Suddenly, I realize the real reason she is calling me two months after our break up. "Oh, I see what's happening here. Now that it didn't work out between you and Chad, you want me back, don't you?"

"Yeah..."

"And you expect me to just get back together with you like nothing ever happened?"

"Well duh, that's like, why I wanted to talk to you. Chad's an ass, he's just a dumb, stuck-up jock and all he wants is..."

"Forget it Lauren!" I've had enough. "You had your chance with me and you blew it. If you loved me the way you said you did, you would have accepted me for who I truly was, whether I was open to you or not. Then this opportunity with Chad comes along, so rather than trying to work things out in our relationship or telling me the truth on your feelings, you just abandon everything, annihilating what we built and cutting me out of your life completely. This is college, not middle school."

"But, but, I really..."

I cut her off. "But nothing!" and hang up the phone.

Five minutes later, my phone receives three consecutive calls from a number that I do not recognize. No voicemail. Hmm... must not be important.

I've got to blow off some steam; that conversation has me heated.

Love Beyond Life

I throw on my hoodie, gather my wallet, keys and iPod, leaving my cell phone behind. I won't need it for this short walk, and quite frankly, I'd rather limit my technological availability to the angels for the next few hours. At a time like this, the only messages I want are those of divine origin. Hence, my iPod =)

Exiting the dorm-room, I take a left, go downstairs, pass a raging open-door party with loud music, beer cans covering the floor and girls dressed for summer. Pressing through a heavy backdoor, I walk outside and stand beneath trees. I look up, spread my arms and take a deep breath.

"Ah!" Nature. Night Nature. Love it.

Taking the iPod out of the pocket of my hoodie, I unwrap the headphones, tuck 'em into my earholes and press play. Naturally, it starts with Angels & Airwaves, on a track called *Epic Holiday* off the new *LOVE* album that Tom made for me the other night while film-scoring my dream in forest.

I listen closely to the song, knowing that it came on first for a reason. The magic of my iPod is that it knows exactly what I need to hear.

No body's right, No body's wrong,

Life's just a game,

It's just one epic holiday.

    (Epic Holiday)

There is nothing I love better than walking around campus at night with my tunes. Perfect solitude. The dimness, the rhythmic glow of street light, the lack of people, the abundance of open space... a man can really get some thinking done.

Passing the amphitheatre, I approach a large rock under a few pine and oak trees, right off the stone pathway. There is an old story about this rock, about a student, Alexandra Seashells, who discovered invisibility here. Legend has it, she just came to this rock and sat down on top of it, turning her attention inward for a few hours. Many students walked passed her, but few were aware of her presence.

When she stood up to walk away, she stepped down with her left foot, then her right foot, and as she took another step with her left, she just vanished. They say it was deliberate, that here at the rock she discovered this ability. Here, she gained this gift.

And rumor has it that even today she appears and disappears all over this campus. She has a ghost-like presence, some would say. But, what changed inside her to make this possible?

Interested in befriending this sacred resonance, and curious if I too am worthy of learning the secret, I hoist myself onto the rock, cross my legs, drop my spine into the perineum and concentrate my focus inward. Staying open to any kind of guidance, I leave my iPod running.

Unpredictable, life's a miracle.
(Some Origins of Fire)

I focus on the space behind my eyes, gazing into the darkness of my eyelids. My breath slows. An energetic force, a morphic resonance, overcomes my body. I give into the Flow.

My fingers find a natural mudra. This must be the morphic template. Templates are like patterns, and the quantum field consists of patterns. Most likely, the number of these patterns is infinite.

When all else fails, sit down, be quiet and let the Flow take you over. Stop stirring the mind; take the spoon out of the pot. Of all possible ways to learn something, this is of highest fidelity. Once you reinforce the innate, human ability of learning from within, you further empower yourself to depend only on your database of quantum consciousness and the Flow as a source of knowledge.

Quantum consciousness is a dynamic pattern of psychic resonances, displayed as various degrees of awareness. The more one focuses inward, the more one's awareness heightens and naturally these psychological tendencies self-purify.

I let the energy and gravity of this sacred resonance take me over. It is so calming, yet so energizing; so filling, yet so empty... I enter bliss.

I become aware now of a light behind my eyelids. No longer is there darkness. It is like I have a night sky within me at the forefront of my brain. The more I gaze into the darkness, the more I realize that there really is no darkness at all.

This light within is like a full moon. So beautiful, so big, so radiant, like an ascending harvest circle on its first few hours.

The light engulfs me. Like the waters before a great wave, the music on my iPod slows and recedes, only to quicken and explode with an intense emotion that can only be described as cobalt blue with a hint of violet.

I transcend sheaths of consciousness, traveling mentally, if not psychically, departing the ordinary Earth plane like a rocket into space.

Blues and golden yellows flash my experience of all that is. I feel myself drifting away, like my mind is slipping out of my body through the top of my head until, finally, I feel no connection to my physical body at all. I am just pure energy, pure ether, pure light.

Tom DeLonge appears to me. "We're going to Thepura, my favorite planet. Come, you have much to learn. Relax yourself as your astral body acclimates to these conditions."

Earth has too many Laurens. Not enough stars. Next stop, Thepura? No objection here.

Chapter Thirteen
Thepura, Land of the Free

After a few minutes of shooting like stars, we arrive at Thepura. It reminds me so much of Earth, but it is more pure, more primal, like Eden. Nature flourishes and civilization is in perfect harmony with it. Everything has been built with a full consciousness of the natural world, every step of the way. I imagine that this is what Earth was like before pollution, before cities, before fear, before knowledge.

It's a beautiful, sunny day here. I look around as the natives walk by. Anyone within ten feet engages me with a smile as they go about their business, exuding a balance between doing their own thing and uplifting those who cross their path. And they all have unusual faces of serenity, like they resonate at a vibration of peace and harmony day in and day out.

But there is more to it; it is not only the natives. There is a peculiar glow about everything here. Not just the people, but the trees, the rocks, the cliffs and that waterfall off in the distance. It all shouts purity.

A waft of pure, loving energy hits me like the sweet fragrance of wild flowers, recharging my core.

"Nice, isn't it?" Tom asks with a smile, unable to hide how happy he is that I am finally here.

"Yeah, totally," I respond with gratitude. "What is this place?"

"It is like Earth, bet better," Tom begins. "Some of the coverts who travel back and forth between here and Earth think of Thepura as Earth's sister planet. The similarities of natural life on both worlds are uncanny. Compare the energy of places like rain forests, deserts, the Himalayan mountain ranges and your Grand Canyon to our best vistas. The energetic signatures are nearly identical, and they all have a like affect on adjacent life forms. They all revive one's spirits and recharge the body in the same way.

"When souls reach a certain level of maturity on Earth, they later have the option to incarnate here, kind of like graduating high school and getting a full-paid scholarship to an elite university. You get to further hone skills you've been developing your whole life with the best of the best." A group of three individuals sending different colored balls of energy to each other in the distance distracts me. I've never seen anything like this.

Out of respect, I direct my attention back to Tom. I'm trying to understand this whole thing. "So people come and go here just like they do back home?"

"Yeah, sort of," He explains. "People come. Souls are certainly born into this world when they are ready for it, and a lot of the mystics on Earth already visit Thepura without ever dying on Earth, just as you are now. It can all be done internally. But unlike Earth, people here never die."

I was starting to grasp it all, but now I'm confused. "But, if people never die, how do you prevent overpopulation and deal with diminishing natural resources?"

Tom chuckles. Apparently I said something funny. "Because Thepurans have the ability to will themselves to any planet. We have absolute freedom; nothing binds a full-blooded Thepuran. We close our eyes, imagine ourselves somewhere else, then BOOM there we are. What advanced meditators on your planet can do with their mind, we can do with our body.

"Wait," I interject. "You're a Thepuran now? What was that whole thing about 'finding planet Heaven' and transfigurverting..." I drift off.

"Well, there's a conversion process that allows for beings like me to dual-process as both angels and Thepurans. It's kinda like if you run an Admin page on facebook. If you want to operate through a different page, you just go up to account on the right, select USE AS..."

"Okay Tom, I get it. Now tell me more about you Thepuran people."

"Haha, alright. We believe in the natural balance of the universe and trust the Flow as intuition guides us to our next destination. This may surprise you, but a lot of our people are actually on Earth right now helping out, preparing for the apocalypse next year... which leads me to why you're here."

"Oh, that secret training thing you've been telling me about, right?" Reminded of the burden, my energy drops slightly, but the buoyancy of this place rebounds and my awareness stays heightened.

"Yes. Come with me."

"Wait, hold on." I back up. "I don't know if I'm ready for this. You still haven't even told me what this 'training' is about. At least give me a hint."

Tom sighs, "It's about fine-tuning the jump-shift. Simply enter the desired reality... the one where your greatest dreams have been actualized, or are in the process of coming to formation. By living in the reality you desire, and feel the most love, your best dreams solidify. In this way of transcendent living, there are no boundaries but those built-up around your imagination."

"So you're going to teach me how to dissolve such mind-forged manacles... how to free my imagination?" My sentence ends on a high note, realizing that I will be forever different.

"Yes. Now come! Time is of the essence."

He puts an arm over my shoulder and we appear in a new area, like beaming back to the starship. We're in a section of Thepura that is of great natural beauty and void of people. We stand beside a large, glass-like pond, overlooked by cliffs of gorgeous purple rock.

Tom raises his arms and the sky turns dark. Clouds densify. Thunder cracks. Rain begins to pour. I am disappointed now; where did our lovely, sunny day go? What is the meaning of this?

"It is your job to learn how to control this," he instructs to me.

"What? I can't control the weather..." I instinctively respond.

Disappointed in my lack of self-confidence, he argues, "You can alter reality, can't you?"

"Yeah, but..." I get cut off.

"But nothing," Tom comes back sternly. "If you can do that, you can do anything. I've seen you, I know what you're capable of, and this is no time for excuses. Now, put your mind to it. Focus. Believe that it is possible. In this moment, you can feel anything you want and do anything you could ever imagine possible. Challenge yourself to make it happen."

Maybe he is right. I'll take a stab at it.

I focus inward. Concentrate. Concentrate. Begin to envision the desired reality, the sunny day we had when we arrived. Remember what it looked like, remember what it felt like. Imagine that, here. Imagine that, now.

And now,
I'll stop the storm if it rains.
I'll light a path far from here.
I'll make your fear melt away,
and the world we know disappear.
(The Gift)

Within myself I find a power. All my attention directs to it. Wait, no. It is not a power; it is an energy. It is the source of my gift. When the energy expresses, it becomes a power, a power that can change reality in any instant. It is like finding a seed within the soil. I see the seed; I know it to be there. All I have to do is provide the right conditions and it will grow.

I nurture the seed of the desired reality. I understand that the sunny day is the next best thing we could experience; I believe it to be so. Of the matrix, it is next in line. We are to shift into it.

"Feel the change within your heart," Tom interjects. "Don't force it; just welcome it. Invite it. Pure love will do the Shift. That's the only thing that ever works."

I listen. I feel. I begin to love how it is a seed full of potential. I give it the option to flourish here and now.

After a moment of uncertainty, not knowing if I am doing this correctly, the seed starts to sprout. It breaks the shell. It grows. Acceleration, exponentially. Just like watching a young bamboo grow in time-lapse...

The reality of storm, rain and cloud dissolves, like smoke dissipating into air. This is different than the sky just clearing up; this is an entire transition from one global matrix to another. We have jump-shifted from one world of possibility to the next. That world has disappeared. A new one begins.

"See, that wasn't so hard, was it?" Tom consoles with a slight smirk.

"No," I realize, still not fully aware of what I had actually done. "I just had to overcome my own cognitive resistance and dig deep to make it happen. I saw the potential like a seed. I nurtured the seed, I loved it, I invited it, just like you said, and it worked. This art is amazing."

"We will do more of this and you will get even better at it. This was just a small storm. Next year you will have something huge to deal with, though, so keep that in the back of your mind. The fate of the Earth rests in your hands. Watch, by the time I'm done with you, you'll be so good at grand ultimate jump-shifting from one world to the next that you'll be doing it in your sleep."

Great, just great, I think. Now, on-top of all my schooling, work-life and social engagement, I will have to do this secret training for hours and hours.

But, Tom makes it out to be very important. Whatever, I can handle it. Like he said, I am capable of anything.

I take a break from all this activity to just sit and enjoy these surroundings. This place is just so beautiful, so vibrant. Everything is full of life; everything is singing. The Thepurans really have something here.

Chapter Fourteen
The Great Moment

The night of December 20th, 2012 came upon us with light speed, rolling into the 21st like nobody's business. Over the past year I have spent a lot of time traveling between here and Thepura, fine-tuning my gift under Tom's guidance. Oh, I also brought Nate Robinson back to the Celtics and we won our 18th championship.

Transitioning into the 21st is arguably the toughest thing humanity has faced yet. Sun spots are firing, water levers are rising, cities disappearing... the world is in chaos.

I sit tight though. I knew this moment would come, and I know exactly what it was that I need to do. I am prepared for what is to be next.

I spend the night meditating silently in my room, waiting. Just patiently waiting. I'm awaiting Tom's command, and he's awaiting mine.

Now, sitting here in all the night's beautiful stillness, with the light I once befriended again gently illuminating my room, as became customary, and my hands in the lotus mudra, he comes to me.

> *If you ask I will do what you say.*
> *All we have is this night to get through...*
>   (The Gift)

According to Tom, all we have to worry about is surviving this one night of extreme chaos. The challenge is an extreme transition.

I have powered down all the technology in my room, cloaked myself in Legacy clothing and consumed plenty of water. *And* my light is with me. I'm good.

The ground below me quakes. I feel the foundation fold. Like a disturbed house of cards, the building caves in. All throughout the building people scream, but I return to an awareness of my breath. I transcend beyond fear.

No longer is there floor beneath me; I am falling. Layers of ceiling crash down on top of me. I am crumbled under rubble. One last piece of material crushes my lungs as I breathe my last breath. I am no more.

> *We're all lost and we're stuck in time.*
> *We feel alone in a strange blue ocean,*
> *And we're all scared as death to die.*
> *(Young London)*

People like I are dying in mass quantities tonight. Unfortunately, some do not know death as well as they should. Some may get stuck in the Earth's astral field. I, however, have been preparing for this death, and know that it is not the end of me.

I have learned how to stay conscious and awake while the body rests. In theory, this shouldn't be that much different. But, it is all put to the test now as my soul wanders the ethers.

I depart now the Earth, traveling up layers of existence and parallel planes. My soul is in limbo, cosmic limbo, and I see others with me. We all travel to a certain, pre-destined location, it seems, like there's a vacuum sucking us all in. The pull is strong. I just go with it.

I see now, though, a light, a star... my star. =) The one that illuminates my room at night, the one that calls to me every time I stand outside beneath the sunless sky... the one that lures me in. I cannot resist. I break the hold of the vacuum. I direct to the star.

I travel to it now.

A feeling of nostalgia overwhelms me. I know this energy. I know this love. I knew it since the night that starlight found its way into my heart. I can't believe that this time, this is how it was destined to happen. Had I a face, I would be crying.

Love Beyond Life

The light is a sign that love will guide you home.
(True Love)

The star greets me as I close in on it. The awareness of what I am as a sentient self shifts. Layers of psychic gunk disperse in the loving presence of this star. It changes the very fabric of my being.

I, too, become light. I regress to a ball of energy. The way light was before life. The way that is evolution, yet in reverse.

I become pure potentiality. The adjacent star continues to nestle me in a force-field of unconditional love.

> *She heard you.*
> *She's a star,*
> *in the nighttime sky.*
> *(True Love)*

Tom, tell me something I don't know.

Together we blend. Her energy becomes mine. My energy becomes hers. Just as wavelengths of blue light superimposed over wavelengths of red light result in a purple that otherwise would not be, so, too, came a new energy of our exchange. We are one, and beautiful at that. This union had been written in the stars all along.

> *With lights and sounds, oh God.*
> *This is such a mess.*
> *And it's like our world,*
> *But we're the last one's left.*
> *And the hair, it stands,*
> *On the back of our necks.*
> *And I swear, it shows,*
> *Heaven must be just like this!*
> (Heaven)

Death is a funny feeling. You have to be ready for it. For me, once I died, I was initially in a cosmic limbo with many other Earth souls. Then, I was called by my star. The closer I came to her, the more alive I felt.

It was all so surreal, like a dream, yet real in a way that is realer than life itself. Without the body and the brain, everything is instantly clear. And here she is now, waking me up from life. With love. See, I knew love had the power to outlast life. Love is a thread connecting everything known and unknown in this universe.

Without a body, this all feels dreamlike. I could really be asleep right now. This could all be in my head, but no. Something tells me I am on the cusp of something epic. There is a clarity to this here experience telling me that this is no dream.

> *I wanna have the same last dream again,*
> *the one where I wake up, and I'm alive.*
> *Just as the four walls close me within,*
> *my eyes are opened up with pure sunlight.*
> (The Adventure)

Her love engulfs me. In this moment, I know beauty, I know truth, and they are inseparable. I feel way too alive to be dreaming. Is this what it feels like to die peacefully? Is this what really happens when we die?

Her loving presence is so comforting. Even though I just lost everything, my life, my family, my friends, my Quantum Resonance term paper, my ninja turtles, I already have everything I could ever want. I am me. I am free. I am here. And on top of all that, she and I are together in an immortal, spiritual way. Lovers of light, illuminating our corner of the galaxy.

By her energy, I know that all is okay in the grand scheme. And I know that I am alive, that I exist, even without a body. Life doesn't take a body; it is the body that takes life.

> *The science is taxing,*
> *I'm waiting for something.*
> *There's images of love and war,*
> *And everything's here to explore.*
> *It's all alike, unusual, a different place but beautiful,*
> *And it is not quite as it seems,*
> *I hear the children's laughs and screams.*
> *(Hallucinations)*

Suddenly it hits me. Earth is gone! And what about all those people? And where is Tom during all of this?! Since the fall-out, I have completely lost connection with him. The last thing I remember is him saying that all we have is this night to get through. Well, I think we've gotten through it, if awakening from death and letting go of Earth is what he meant.

But why haven't I seen him since then? Oh wait, I get it. Maybe I no longer need him now. I have his music forever in my heart, and that is all I will need from this point forward.

I feel something tugging me from a distance, pulling me in a certain direction. It is the same feeling I had when I was getting sucked away with all those other Earth souls earlier. Some unknown force rips me away from my long lost lover. This sears. As we separate, a void fills within. Examining it more closely, I recognize it to be the same mysterious void I found while meditating on Earth. The void Buddhists speak of~ the emptiness.

I now travel in an upcurrent with other vibrational sentients, presumably from the Earth fall-out as well. Were shall all these souls go?

I'm flying, and something's reaching out.
Vibrations, can you hear them now?
Please help us, we're running out of time...

(Flight of Apollo)

All these souls are in need of help. They don't know what is happening. I sense that they feel lost and powerless, confused and aimless. There's gotta be something I can do.

Just like on Earth, I default to my breathing. It is not easy, now that I no longer have a body, but I give it my best shot.

I inhale the way a star would breathe. Take in the environment. Become one with it. Know it as yourself. I feel their essence enter.

As everyone else, I have fear and confusion. I trace now the root of that fear and confusion to a source that is untended compassion. Holding the seed, I breathe into it. It grows, just as did the new world on Thepura.

The compassion spreads like wildfire. I feel the sentients around me soften. They relax. They remember what it is like to die.

They begin to accept the fact that all is lost, that Earth is over. Soon they shall begin life anew on some other planet and learn some other lesson uniquely suited to their own spiritual journey.

Perhaps that is the reason I was pulled away. Perhaps I just needed to help all these lost souls. I don't care what pulled me away, though, because I am the one steering this ship. I go where I want to go. It's my life. I do what I want. 'Nough said. I am me. I am free, remember?

I am going back to her!

Getting the hang of traveling at light speed in this rainbow body, I zoom towards her. Finding the direction is not hard. I could recognize that light of hers anywhere!

I again come close to her. Yet she is a star, and I am a star in the shape of a human, roughly. This light body is not easy to explain.

I want to reach out and touch the light that she is. I want to feel her more deeply. She is just so inviting; I cannot resist.

I do it. I extend my left arm and enter the light. Just as she touched my heart that one night, I do now the same to her. I find her core, the inner pulsation. She turns pink, then purple.

This is a cosmic transformation. She materializes into a bodily form similar to my own. Wow, she is more beautiful than I remember her being that time by the waterfall. But the look in her eyes is the same, exactly the same. Different house, different window, but same soul.

We can now speak words to each other, but no, that is not important. This first kiss will say everything, and more.

> *Stars fall like dust,*
> *Our lips will touch,*
> *We speak too much.*
> *(Breathe)*

Love Beyond Life

The instant our lips touch, the void inside, that formed during our separation, bursts into a galaxy, all on its own. Gases and planets, solars and stellars, spew forth from what I once thought was emptiness.

Oh, so this is how galaxies are formed.

Here comes LOVE, our soundtrack.

> *Night gets better,*
> *And wait, so wonderful,*
> *They move together*
> *And dance, so colorful.*
> *Kiss like flowers*
> *That breathe with pheromones.*
> *Songs get louder,*
> *It feels so natural.*
> *(Young London)*

I open my eyes a little to see Tom hovering in the distance, along with several other angels, all being witness to us, as if this were a unique moment in cosmic history. See, I knew Tom could never be far off. Disregarding onlookers, I return to amplifying our true love.

Here I am,
And here we go,
Life's waiting to begin.
　　　(The Adventure)

With death comes life. With loss comes gain. This is the way of the universe, and to desire anything different would go against the grain of all that has ushered us into existence thus far. It took the history of the entire universe to make this current moment, so why not embrace it?

This is Flow. If this is not God, I don't know what is.

Feeling this with her, this new galaxy between us, and how encouraged we are by the angels, I know this is not the end. No, it can't be. I feel we're just beginning.

We are one, and we are two. We are none, and we are all. We are beautiful. We are great. We are for you to relate.

For lives that are bitter, death is bittersweet. For lives that are sweet, death is even sweeter. Life, death... no difference. Awake, asleep... no difference. Earth, no Earth... no difference.

Humans are silly. Clinging to their lives, clinging to their world. For what? Everything comes and goes. That is Nature at its finest. If we lose it all, do we not gain? If we are empty, are we not full? If we die, do we not live on?

Please, do you really think the universe would tease us with moments of absolute happiness and contentment, only to blow out the flame that is our soul later on? The highest human emotions are so enlivening and invigorating because they are not human; they are spiritual; they are of our immortal nature. They are of the great timelessness~ the Quantum Now. Because we are now, we shall forever be.

This is our destiny; it has pulled us together. Destiny is a strand of quantum energy. It acts as a guiding force, bridging together possible realities. Through a sequence of life experiences, the matrix presents itself in linear time, but ultimately, time functions on a cyclical, orbital or even galactic framework. The stream of consciousness accounts for linear ways of thinking, believing and living. The ocean of consciousness, however, accounts for the transcendent, quantum reality.

This easily explains inspiration, intuition and radical new ideas. Fragments of a more evolved consciousness resonate from the future to the present by way of the quantum field. What is once in the quantum field will always be in the quantum field; nothing is ever lost, and everything that will be known can be, here and now.

We cycle through selective resonances and in this manner transcend linear consciousness. Our best possible future beckons for us to take steps in a positive direction, if we can only listen for the messages and strike while the iron is hot.

All that time I'd been looking for her, only to find that she had been with me all along. She was the star in the sky always distracting my attention, always watching over me, patiently waiting for me to remember.

Welcome love in any way it presents itself. For, without love, how are we to know that this is life, this here moment, is real? I have never seen anything more magnificent than the way humans love one another. So giving, so selfless, so Godlike.

Where else in the universe do you see someone give up all they have, all they've accumulated for years and years, risk things they have spent their whole lives working on and achieving, just so that another may have an easier battle? Where else do you see such risk? No where but Earth.

Earth, hmm. I miss it already. I know it is not perfect. It has negative emotion, hardship, pain, suffering, and the like, but it is not that bad of a place. For me, and another seven billion odd number of souls, it was a perfect fit. It was home.

Chapter Fifteen
Perfect

Still in the ethers, she caresses my face, bringing me back to her. I remember now what it is like to be human, a fearful lover rather than a loving fearer. This whole time, she was the only thing I was afraid of. Not having her... having the emptiness inside... never really knowing love. That was my only fear.

    I exhaust. Black. Pitch.

I'd like to say,

That you're my only fear

And when I dream,

It slowly disappears,

And when I wake,

I'm right here by your side

To feel your heart

Beat in and out of time.

    (Call to Arms)

"Wake up, wake up, wake up!"

Sunshine. Birds chirping. I have sensation again of a physical body, and I am lying down in my own bed at school, back in the same room that caved in last night. I open my eyes to see her gazing into mine, the way I did at her in the sky every night. My heart overflows in happiness, spilling all over the floor; I don't know what this is, or how I ended up back here. And I especially don't know how she came back with me!

"You did it!" Lauren says, excitedly, as if she'd been awake for hours, patiently waiting, watching my face for the moment I regained consciousness to say that very line.

"Did what?" I say, confused.

"Brought me back. You brought us all back!"

"What? But I didn't even..."

Tom appears to me and me alone. "I told you, man, you'll get so good at grand ultimate jump-shifting that you will do it in your sleep."

Wow, really? Unreal. Un Flippin' Real. I look at him and smile as air compresses from my stomach and out through my nostrils. Had I more energy, I'd be filling the room with laughter. No way, no bloody way.

> *A perfect life*
> *For a perfect brand new day,*
> *And you're the next in line.*
> (Valkyrie Missile)

The bigger issue to me, though, is how Lauren dual-processed as both a human and a star.

"But Lauren, how did you..."

"What, you think you're like, the only one that can bend space and time to your will?"

"Kinda... but, but, how could you have been both here and also up there?"

"How could I not have been?" Fresh, in a cute way. "We live in a quantum reality. Didn't you say that time was just a permeable surface?"

Look at that. Beaten at my own game. I roll back over in bed. I don't believe this. Lauren, my soulmate all along?

She doesn't give up. "I was a star in the sky because that's what happened to me after the Earth fallout... but like, that in no way stopped me from illuminating your past, as it unfolded in a present moment, years before the fallout, to get your attention, in a way you never would have guessed. I had to remind you of the love I truly feel for you, and help you shift us back."

"What the hell is this! Tom dual-processes as an angel and a Thepuran, you lived on Earth and in the sky as a star at the same time... and all I can do is cultivate worlds. This isn't fair."

"Tom? Who's that?" She questions.

I laugh. "I'll tell you later."

Unlike Ros Well, Lauren can speak up about her mate being too reserved, as she broke up with me for not being open. And unlike Oem, I can give a woman the attention she needs to feel loved and appreciated. We both have grown; this time, things will be more balanced.

I guess I wished so strongly to be with her once again that one night under the stars that, once I found her in the spirit world, in that trans-dimensional reality layered over our physical one, even though I didn't recognize my star to be Lauren, my subconscious began creating for ourselves a new world.

I have awakened in a world much similar to the one left behind. People again roam the Earth and do what they please. This is a world where 2012 was no apocalypse; no, it was an enlightened transformation.

Sadly, though, few will ever know the reality of reality, the truth that we all did die, fallen to our folly, and have now come back as if doomsday never happened. But oh well. This is the same thing that happened when I brought Super Shredder back into my life. The truth that is relevant only to I, the creator of my world.

There is a part of her I will never know, but that is what makes it love. Love of an unknown that is safe to explore~ a journey within between two people that never gets old, that can never be exhausted. To find this mystery within another and explore it passionately, boundlessly, and tenderly~ that is the purpose of life.

We are here to learn to love, and not just how to love, but how to love deep. The stars guide us all, just as they did for me. In darkness, asleep or awake, we are most connected to our true lover, whether we know it or not. For we, as beings of light, shine to heal, illuminate and enlighten one another.

There is no love without others. We exist to share energy, to evolve each other, and do so by loving. The more we love, the lighter we become.

In relationships we are co-dependent. They need us and we need them. We cannot lead lives of isolation; existence ceases to self- validate. For enlightenment, seek first within yourself and then without yourself. Master your relationship with the outside world. When you love it, it loves you back. I now know that true love and enlightenment come hand in hand. You cannot experience one without the other. Such is the way of the human condition. So beautiful. So perfect. So great.

This love operates beyond life. Life cannot contain it, for all life exists as a fragment of this grand love. Everything, from here to the far reaches of space, is love. Intuitively we may know this, but it takes the connection with oneself and another to experience this.

Yes, Lauren broke my heart, but heartbreak is an opportunity to then share yourself in more ways than one. Focus on the feelings of love you once felt. All those feelings came from within; love comes from within oneself and projects out into the world. When you felt love from another, it was simply because the love you were putting out into the world was reflected back to you, just as beauty is in the eye of the beholder.

Yes, they love us, and we feel that, but we would feel nothing if at first we did not initially love them. It takes love to know love.

It is the way love bounces that we experience the world and consequently exist. We can learn to jump-shift, to transcend from one realm to another, but all that is irrelevant if we realize that simply talking to people and forming new relationships is a natural way of entering new worlds.

Take a risk. Talk to a complete stranger. Finally spark up a conversation with that girl in class who has always caught your eye, as did I. You never know.

Made in the USA
Lexington, KY
16 January 2014